By Eva Muñoz

The Last Laugh

Published by DSP PUBLICATIONS
www.dsppublications.com

EVA MUÑOZ

The Last Laugh

DSP PUBLICATIONS

Published by

DSP PUBLICATIONS

5032 Capital Circle SW, Suite 2, PMB# 279, Tallahassee, FL 32305-7886 USA
http://www.dsppublications.com/

The Last Laugh
© 2022 Eva Muñoz

Cover Art
© 2022 L.C. Chase
http://www.lcchase.com
Cover content is for illustrative purposes only and any person depicted on the cover is a model.

Trade Paperback ISBN: 978-1-64108-325-6
Digital ISBN: 978-1-64108-324-9
Trade Paperback published February 2022
v. 1.0

Printed in the United States of America
∞
This paper meets the requirements of
ANSI/NISO Z39.48-1992 (Permanence of Paper).

CHAPTER ONE

Dina

ASK ANYONE what their greatest dream is, and more often than not the answer you'll get is to travel the world. In a recent survey, travel was listed in the top three leisure activities of people in America. And when someone comes into money, what's the thing they do after they buy the expensive car and the extravagant house? They travel.

Let's not forget all those travel extravaganza prizes you see on the *Wheel of Fortune*. You name it. From a once-in-a-lifetime trip to Paris or an all-expenses-paid family vacation to the happiest place on earth, I've curated it all. You won't believe how many times I answered the phone to someone wanting the exact package mentioned on some game show or another.

There isn't a person in the world who doesn't have aspirations of seeing the Eiffel Tower or walking the Great Wall of China or taking the Haunted Mansion ride at Disneyland—when it's operational, anyway. Anyone who works hard treats themselves to a vacation at least once a year if they can afford it. There are so many promos now that it's as easy as clicking a button. You'll be on a plane in no time.

I'm on a call with a client early Thursday morning assisting with just that—making travel arrangements. You might say, "But Dina, with the internet, why would someone still call a travel agency for assistance? Isn't your line of work moot at this point?"

First of all, I'll have to commend you on the use of the word "moot." Second of all, yes, the internet has made my work a dying art form. But we travel agents are still a necessary service for those who don't know how to book a flight via the airline website of their choice.

At the same time, we provide packages. You don't have to think of a single thing when you book your plans with us. We even give you the best perks and travel insurance. How can you beat that?

Like seventy-six-year-old Mrs. Miller, who's booking an all-expenses-paid European adventure package for her granddaughter because she's graduating valedictorian. Mrs. Miller wants round-trip tickets at a reasonable price with hotel accommodations and a suite of guided tours.

I'd like to see you book an eight-country, multiple-city tour with connections that will take you from London all the way to Switzerland and back in a month. Like I said, it's an art form. I need to make sure that everything interconnects or I will have lost a seventeen-year-old abroad and Mrs. Miller will be very upset.

"Okay, Mrs. Miller, the itinerary for Jemma is all set. Would you like me to email it to you?" I ask, clicking into my agent mode and forgetting for a moment that the woman doesn't have email.

"Can you mail it to me, dear?" she says in the nicest voice.

I honestly want her to be my grandmother. I'm just not sure she'll take kindly to the fact that I eat pussy instead of dick. I sigh inwardly.

I wish I had someone who would buy me an all-expenses-paid tour of Europe. Sometimes I hate my job. I get to create these elaborate dream vacations for people without actually being able to go to the places I book for them. At least, not until I make partner at the agency. Partners get invited to all the best places—for free, I might add—in order to better promote them when a traveler asks.

For once I want to see the Mediterranean and maybe even swim in it. I'd certainly look good topless along the beaches of southern France. Maybe I'll even meet a nice French girl who will school me in French Kissing 101. Even if I'm proficient, I wouldn't mind a master's degree.

Unfortunately, there's a slight snag to my making partner—you need to be a member of a club I'm not part of. Mind you, it's not really a requirement… because that would involve HR. It's more like a reality, and I'm currently lacking in that department.

"Okay, Mrs. Miller, I'll have everything printed out and overnighted to you. I've also taken the liberty of preboarding your granddaughter so all she needs to do is show up at the airport and check in her luggage."

"Oh, that's mighty nice of you, Dina. My Jemma will be so happy when I give her this gift."

"It's my pleasure, Mrs. Miller. Thank you for booking with us at Sunset Vacations. We are always happy to serve you." I pause. "Should you need anything else, please don't hesitate to call. You have my direct line."

"I might just take that cruise I've always been wanting to go on."

I smile. "I'm just one call away. I'll have you breathing in that sea air in no time."

"I'm sure you will. Thank you, dear."

I slump in my seat the moment the call ends. So early on a Thursday and already I envy a girl who could have been my daughter. Good thing I figured out early in my life that I'm a muff diver and someone uninclined to breed. One day I'll find a bumper sticker that says *Honk if you like pussies* and drive around proudly.

Leaning forward, I cover my face with both hands and say to myself over and over again, "I love my job. I love my job. I love my job."

"Good," my boss says behind me. "Can you step into my office for a moment, Ms. Oliver?"

Startled, I jump off my seat and slip on my heels. I don't think this day can get any worse for me. Envy is a horrible feeling to have in your gut before lunch. It's like drinking a soda without eating anything. The acid eats away at your stomach lining, giving you the sensation of popping bubbles running up your throat.

Wishing that the pencil skirt I wore today had an adequate slit, I teeter into my boss's office. He gestures at the door and I close it behind me. Then he points at one of the chairs opposite from where he sits behind his desk.

Behind him stand shelves filled with every award imaginable. Sunset Vacations couldn't have stayed competitive without Bob at the helm. Want to go around the world? Bob's your guy. Even I find myself weak at the knees just thinking of the logistics of planning a tour package that massive. He can do it in his sleep.

Speaking of starting to feel weak at the knees, and grateful I don't have to stand the entire time—stilettos aren't exactly the most comfortable shoe choice, but they do make my legs look a mile long—I take a seat. Just because I sit at a desk all day doesn't mean I can't dress like a jet-setter ready to hop onto a private plane and sip champagne. "Always dress for success, Dina," my pops drilled into me every chance he got.

"Is something the matter, Bob?" I ask, breaking the silence that's stretched out a little too long. At this point, I would have been checking if the line was cut if I were on a call.

"Did I just hear you book an entire European trip?" he asks, eyeing me intently.

"Yes. Thirty days, eight countries."

"The commission on that is—"

"Quite substantial," I say, cutting him off.

I'm already planning what I'm going to do with that money. It's going to my dream vacation fund. Or several pairs of ridiculously expensive shoes. I haven't decided yet.

"Good. I always said you were my best agent."

"I try to do what I can to please the client, sir." I nod. "Can I know what you called me here for?"

"Always direct to the point."

"My desk is unmanned." I hike my thumb over my shoulder. "I'd hate to miss an incoming call."

It means business, and Bob knows that. The more commissions I make, the better. It's a win-win for the both of us.

"I'm guessing you know what time of the year it is?" he asks.

Of course I remember. It's the time of year when the partners fly off on a sponsored retreat. A travel-agent open house, if you will, where they get to experience a new resort, hotel, or travel destination. It's one of the reasons why agents like myself grab at any opportunity to become partner. But I don't say any of that. Instead, I sit at the edge of my seat.

My throat closes. Is this it? The moment I've been waiting for?

"Well, we were really impressed by your work," he says, prolonging my torture. Is he going to say what I think he's about to say? "Which is why I'd like you to be the one to confirm all the details of the trip."

In my head I'm doing cartwheels and dancing the Running Man until his words actually sink in. "You...." I have to convince my mouth to actually work to form the proper words. "You want me to plan the trip?"

My heart sinks. I don't know what I was thinking. Certainly not that they'd make me partner or anything.

He shakes his head. "Chateau Blanc has graciously invited us to stay and experience what they call a romantic lifestyle. Everything has already been planned. I just need someone I can rely on to make sure all the details are correct. The names of partners, the tickets, the reservations. You know the drill."

Oh, I know the drill, all right. I swallow down the massive rock of emotion that's formed in my throat and manage to cobble together a decent smile. "I can certainly do that for you."

Bob nods. "Good. Can it be ready by the time we all meet at Bar Rafael this evening?"

I make the mental calculations. Four partners plus their spouses. It will mean having lunch at my desk and forwarding all my calls to someone else. I bite the inside of my cheek.

"It's doable," I say.

"Perfect." Bob flashes a blinding smile. "Make sure to bring the details over to me. We'll discuss them over drinks."

Drinks. Sure. Some consolation prize that is.

Fate is such a fickle bitch. She dangles what I want most in front of me but then yanks it just out of reach. Unable to maintain my carefully constructed unaffected mask of professionalism much longer, I push up off the chair and stand.

"If you don't need anything else...?" I start backing toward the door, which isn't easy in a pencil skirt and sky-high stilettos. "I'll get right on confirming those travel details for you."

"Go get 'em, Tiger."

I hate that he calls me Tiger. It's so condescending. But he is also the man who holds my dream of traveling the world in the palms of his hands. I need to knock this one out of the park. Then he'll see my value as a partner in this agency.

I hurry to my seat and kick off my shoes. I pick up the phone and call one of the other agents to let them know I'll be transferring my calls to them. Once that's done, I order a salad from the nice lady who brings her sandwich cart into the office, and get to work.

DRINKS AT Bar Rafael is a weekly hang for everyone at Sunset Vacations. I'm not sure when it first started, but Bob encouraged it as a way for the agents and partners to socialize outside of work. For the company to succeed, everyone must function as a team. "Think of it as a bonding exercise," Bob told me when I first started as an assistant straight out of college.

Attendance isn't mandatory, but not showing up does send the wrong message. Not that anyone ever misses a meetup. Going to a bar to unwind after a hard day is just what the doctor ordered. I think that's why Bob picked the end of the week for a casual get-together.

And what a great place to hang out. Bar Rafael boasts the best cocktails and the finest selection of whiskey in the city. For New York? That's saying something.

With the folder of travel details safely tucked under my arm, I push through the door. Merry cheer and glasses clinking greet me, along with a soft smooth jazz piped in from invisible speakers on the ceiling.

The hardwood floors and handsome bar speak of elegance. The moss-green leather booths and stools combine vintage with cozy comfort. Every bottle of alcohol worth having lines an entire wall, spanning one end of the space to the other.

Perfume, aftershave, and musky notes of cedar commingle in the air. My favorite bartender spots me from a mile away. I already sent him my order via text right as I left our office. He pushes a Grey Goose martini to me.

I slide a crisp twenty his way and pick up the glass. He tilts his head toward the booth at the back where the partners have gathered. They start the evening amongst themselves; then they adjourn and mingle.

I take a sip from my drink, the orange bitters and the subtle nut and pepper flavors of the vodka giving me the courage I need. I catch the tail end of a conversation between Bob and one of the partners.

"Parker's already been packing for a week, and still he's not done." Bob shakes his head.

"My wife's the same way." The partner chuckles. "She's already bought an entirely new wardrobe for this trip."

They all laugh.

"These couples' retreats are always the highlight of my travel calendar," another partner says.

An idea clicks in my mind. If there's any chance of me making partner, then I have to take it. I start speaking before common sense overrides my brain.

"You're lucky," I say. "My fiancée always waits until the last minute to pack for a trip."

As one, all the heads of the partners swivel toward me. I pause, martini in hand. The intimidation brought about by the attention of all the best travel agents in the business borders on overwhelming. It's an unseen force that can knock you over.

I, on the other hand, take one more sip and stand my ground. This is it. The lie is out there.

Bob eyes me with interest. "You never told me you have a fiancée, Ms. Oliver." His gaze travels to my ring finger.

I fight a blush and think fast. "It's new. So new, in fact, that we don't even have rings yet."

"Ah, one of those spur-of-the-moment proposals," the last of the partners fills in, much to my relief. "Those are the most romantic."

I go with it. "Exactly."

"Is that the travel itinerary I asked you to finalize?" Bob asks, indicating the folder tucked away at my side.

"Oh yes." I use my free hand to pull it from my side.

The partners look to Bob, and a silent communication that I don't quite understand happens between all of them. In my mind, I'm scrambling. Have they seen through my lie? Will they expose me for the charlatan that I am?

The thought of getting fired sends a chill down my spine. I shouldn't have opened my mouth. I thought that by mentioning a fiancée I'd fit in with the partners. That they'd see me as someone capable of joining their ranks.

Instead, they stand and leave me alone with Bob.

Normally I'd think nothing of this since Bob said we'd discuss the travel details over drinks. Yet the shift in the air from convivial to serious says otherwise.

"Join me?"

The question sounds more like a statement than a request. I slide into the now vacant side of the booth and hand over the folder. Bob flips it open and starts scanning the pages.

"Remind me again, Ms. Oliver, how long have you been working with Sunset?" Bob asks, keeping his eyes on the folder and the papers within.

"A little…." I clear my throat and start over. "A little over seven years."

"And in those seven years, I trust that you've found fulfilment in what you do?"

The question takes me by surprise, but the answer comes quicker than a snap. "I love it."

"Even if it's hard work?"

"Even so." I take a deep breath and let it out nice and slow. "Being able to put together a trip that I'm sure the client has been yearning for brings me so much joy."

The corners of Bob's lips lift slightly. "And what is the best part of this job?"

Again, the answer comes to me without an ounce of hesitation. "Surprising the client with the unexpected. A perk they didn't know about. Or adding a tour to their itinerary that I know they will love. It's like I'm taking the trip with them."

Even if that's far from the case. I plan the trips. But one day I will finally take them.

Bob nods. "This is great work."

I lean forward. "I made sure to organize everything from pickup to airport drop-off and luggage check-in. All the first-class tickets have been confirmed. And I've spoken to the liaison officer over at Chateau Blanc to make sure airport pickup will be there as soon as you land at Charles de Gaulle Airport."

To a client on the phone, I'd be using the abbreviation, which is CDG, but I just love saying the name of the Paris airport. Charles de Gaulle. It has such an elegant ring to it.

"I never doubted your skill," Bob says. "You remind me so much of myself when I was first starting out."

My heart swells. "Thank you. That means a lot coming from you."

"That being said, there is one more slot on this trip," he continues. "I'd like for you and your fiancée to join us."

I almost slip off the edge of the booth. "Sir?"

"I assume this will not be a problem?"

"Of—of course not." My throat dries for a whole different reason. "My fiancée is just out of the state on a business trip, but I expect her to be back soon. She'll be overjoyed about the idea. Again, thank you, sir."

"Make sure to add yourself and your fiancée to the itinerary." Bob grins. "It's going to be one romantic trip."

On jelly legs, I manage to stand and make my way back to the bar. My favorite bartender is already placing another martini in front of me. I slump into the seat.

"You don't look so good," he says.

I huff into my second drink. "You wouldn't know where I could find a fiancée on short notice, would you?"

He laughs, thinking I'm joking. I should have known my lie would bite me in the butt. I need to find myself a fiancée. Shouldn't be hard, right? If only these things could be arranged online....

CHAPTER TWO

Claire

COMEDY IS a funny thing, and I don't mean that as a joke. It's the kind of lifestyle you don't think about until you're standing on stage for what seems like the hundredth time and you actually get your first standing O. It doesn't get addictive until you get your first laugh.

Weird thing is? I wasn't the funny kid in school. I was the shy one, content to be by herself. I had friends, sure. But I'm not the life of the party by any means.

In my yearbook it actually says *Most Forgettable*. Yeah. That's what it says. Not that I did anything particularly memorable. Basically, I went to school and then I went home. Rinse and repeat. I don't even think they remembered I belonged to the graduating class until I took my yearbook photo. Sad but true.

Well, now I'm doing something that's worth remembering. I sure showed them. They don't call me the Taylor Swift of comedy for nothing. Not the fame—not yet, anyway. Still working on that. More like my content.

I tell jokes about my exes for a living. My parents barely talk to me because of it. Let's not even discuss the fact that I'm a lesbian. That they can tolerate. But become a comedian? Good luck.

"Yeah," I tell the audience at the Funny Bone, a comedy club downtown. "My parents wanted me to be a doctor."

I get a couple of groans, the usual reaction when I start down this road.

"I gave it the good college try, I really did," I say. "Unfortunately, I was more there for the hot interns than the studying. When I started trading giving head for copying assignments, I knew something had to change."

A chorus of laughter follows my punch line. My style of comedy follows my life experiences. Mostly the myriad of girlfriends who have come and gone. The more complicated the better. Back when I was starting out, I was what they called a topical comic, meaning if there was something happening right that moment, I made a joke about it.

Well, try doing that when nothing particularly interesting is happening. Not so funny then. I totally bombed. Then I started talking about this one ex I broke up with at the time. The laughs I got changed the trajectory of my career. For the better, really.

So I revamped my act. I looked at the comics I admired and saw they were talking about their life and their experiences. That was easy enough to do. I turned my inner pain into situations that made others laugh.

Pretty soon after that, the clubs I went to for sets started getting packed. There were some nights when the club owners would beg me for another show because there was still a line around the block waiting to see me. That totally blew my mind.

"I dated a girl once who didn't eat carbs," I say, moving into my closing joke.

Already the crowd is laughing.

"What? Didn't think I dated girls, or didn't think because of my juicy candy thighs that I'd be able to give up eating carbs just to date someone?"

The question gets me more laughs. This is good.

My show is called Fat, Fun, and Single because I'm all three of those things. But I prefer to call myself Rubenesque. Yes, I'm on the heavy side, but I can still fit into those sexy skinny jeans. Now, if only I was a little taller than my five foot three, I'd be golden.

"So I was dating her, and you guessed it, I stopped eating carbs. It was getting that serious between us."

I put two fingers to my lips and stick my tongue in between them. I get the typical whistles and hollers at that. The crowd tonight is awesome, and I'm on fire.

"We're getting all hot and heavy, but what she doesn't know is that I've been sneaking bites of bread at night when she's asleep. Because come on…." I trace my curves with the hand not holding the mic. "I got to maintain these rolls, baby."

I get cheers.

"Yeah, I was eating rolls at that time too."

More laughter. One lady in front spits out her drink she's laughing so hard. Her friend smacks her back several times as she lapses into a coughing fit. She's my kind of audience member. If someone isn't red in the face by the end of the night, I consider it a failure on my part.

"Anyway, one night after we make sweet, sweet love...." I pause for the cheers and jeers. "I wait a couple of minutes to make sure she's asleep, and I tiptoe to the kitchen to visit my mistress. They were having a sale on white bread that day."

The roar of laughter is like a wave coming at me. It's a total rush. I can feel it like sparks underneath my skin.

"As I take a bite of the bread, the lights come on. I'm caught with my mouth deep into this slice. My then girlfriend says to me, 'You're cheating on me with bread?' To which I respond, 'Honey, it's not you, it's me. I really like bread.' She narrows her eyes at me and says, 'More than me?' I looked from her to the bread and I knew I had to make a decision. I broke up with her that night."

The crowd leaps up and starts clapping, the inside of the club going wild.

I raise my hand and say, "That's it for me. My name's Claire Rox. Good night!"

I walk off the stage while the entire room is still on their feet. It's a heady feeling to know you have them in the palm of your hand. I wouldn't give up doing comedy for anything.

The other performers that night come up and congratulate me. I take in all their adulation. Some of them, I know, are genuine. The rest are green with envy.

I don't mind. They want to be where I am. That's understandable. It's part of the gig.

I head into the greenroom at the back to get my stuff. My phone rings right as my hand closes around my bag. I fish it out and my eyes beam at the sight of my agent's name.

This is it. The call I've been waiting all night for. A bout of nerves tingle in my stomach. I take a couple of steadying breaths before I answer. "Hey, Dwight," I say. "How's it hanging?"

"How did the show go?" he asks. It's a usual question. He's the one responsible for my career, after all.

"Murdered."

"That's what I like to hear." Then a pause. "I've got some bad news."

Remember the nerves in my stomach? Well, they just became rocks.

I puff out a breath and say, "I didn't get in."

"Maybe next year."

"That's what you said last year."

Look. I'm an entertainer. You'd think that I would be used to rejection by now. I mean, we get rejected on an almost daily basis. Hell, I created an entire act about being rejected and being the one doing the rejecting. But I've always wanted to be a part of the Edinburgh Comedy Festival. It's the gateway to the world.

It opens up a chance to participate in Just For Laughs in Toronto. And from there I can move on to selling out theaters and not just clubs. Then from there? Arenas, baby!

How long do I have to wait to take my career to the next level? I certainly have the comedy chops. I kill every damn night.

"I do have an audition for you if you're interested," Dwight says. "The production is even willing to fly you out to LA."

"You know acting isn't my thing," I say.

"It's a way to get your foot in the door, Claire."

Dwight keeps insisting that if I make it in acting it will boost my comedy career. Sure. Chris Rock did it. Kevin Hart too. But as much as possible, that's not the route I want to take. I want acting to be a last resort.

Then the thought hits me. What if this *is* my last resort? Do I have it in me to wait another year for a chance at Edinburgh? What if all my chances dry up and I'm forever stuck playing clubs?

A shudder runs through me. "Give me time to think about it?"

"You have until next week," he says, hope clear in his tone.

"All right. Next week it is."

I hang up the phone, stuff it in my back pocket, and leave my stuff in the greenroom. I head from backstage to the bar. I need one giant stiff drink. Or two.

CHAPTER THREE

Dina

WHEN I was a little girl, I got really good at hide-and-seek. It was so much fun finding the right hiding place, because if you're not found, you win. And I always won. I think a part of my competitive streak comes from that experience.

One time, my friends and I gathered to play. The second one of the girls started counting down, I went in search of my hiding spot. Somehow, I knew they'd never look up. So instead of going far, I climbed the tree my friend used to lean against during the countdown.

I totally won the game that day. They searched high and low for me. Even the girls who were already found joined in on looking for me. Only my uncontrollable giggles gave me away in the end. Ah, I miss those days.

Adults play a game of hide-and-seek too. There are several versions of this. One, you call in sick. Two, you hide in the staff room. Three, you pretend to be busy.

The third example is what I employ as a way to avoid any more questions about my fiancée from Bob.

Of course, that doesn't stop the itinerary of the couples retreat from magically appearing in my inbox by the end of the next day. There's no hiding from walking tours of the town where the chateau is located. A personalized orientation of the resort. A day at the vineyard, complete with wine tasting. Oh my! I read each and every item with the gusto of a starving man at a buffet.

The next email contains information about Chateau Blanc, located in the picturesque Loire Valley. It was built in two phases by architects Philibert de l'Orme and Jean Bullant in the mid-sixteenth century. According to the chateau's history, Henry II's mistress Diane de Poitiers oversaw everything. Over the centuries, the palace became the property of a number of notable women, including Catherine de' Medici. Its new owners saw the potential of the space and made it the premier resort it is today, providing many couple-centric activities.

The last email asks for the complete information of my fiancée. This is so Bob can send everything to Chateau Blanc and all the arrangements can be made. My stomach tumbles. How can I send information that doesn't exist?

"I'm so getting fired," I whisper under my breath.

That's when shit gets real for me. I pack up my desk, shut down my computer, and call it a day. I need to find a fiancée ASAP.

I might be crafty, but I'm not that duplicitous. I'd like to maintain a shred of dignity, please. Anyway, I don't think I can fake having fun with someone who's not actually there with me. Why did I have to say fiancée? It makes things so much more complicated.

It's going to involve staring lovingly into each other's eyes. Lots of hugging. And a kiss or two just to make it look like we are truly in love. How the hell am I supposed to pull that off when I'm currently as single as a yolk in an egg? Although, my mom did say finding a double-yolked egg brought good luck. Right now? I need all the luck I can get.

I'm both excited and terrified at this new stage of my life. To the point where every time I think about it, I actually feel the need to pee. I'm racking my brain on how to accomplish this without being seen as the total liar that I am.

Oh, who am I kidding? I'm going to have to smoke-and-mirrors this shit. I've bullshitted my way out of many things in my life—a speeding ticket, jury duty, a class photo because my outfit just wasn't right—but this might be my biggest challenge yet.

Can I actually get on that plane sans a fiancée and get away with it? What if I do a good enough job representing the agency? Would they forgive me for lying about my relationship status?

In an ideal world, I would go on this trip, schmooze the other partners, and make an amazing impression on our hosts. I can see it now. My boss kissing the ground I walk on while I strike a power pose like the lesbian Superman.

Sadly for me, we don't live in an ideal world, do we? If I go on this trip without a fiancée, I could get spectacularly fired. Not only would I be out of a job, they might even ask me to pay back all the money they spent. And that's not going to come cheap, because it's a trip of a lifetime experience. Calculating the expenses makes my head spin.

I grab my jacket and my purse and leave. When I reach street level, I breathe in for what seems like the first time since leaving Bar Rafael last night. My shoulders are totally in knots as I begin to walk.

I can do this. I will find a solution that will get me everything I want. I'm not about to let this opportunity slip away over the lack of a fiancée.

As I cross the street, I notice a flier taped to a post. The picture of a woman on a stage catches my attention. I take down the flier and look over it. My eyebrows rise.

"The Fat, Fun, and Single comedy show with Claire Rox," I say to myself.

Something about this Claire Rox intrigues me. I can't stop staring at her picture. There's a charisma about her that I feel even through a flier.

She certainly *looks* like she's a lot of fun. Her smile alone could melt hearts. And as the title of her show promises, she's gorgeously curvy. She's the type of woman who makes an impression.

Single? I find that hard to believe. But it's certainly interesting. What I know for sure is I want to know more about this Claire Rox.

It says on the flier that her show is all about her exes. I'm not a stranger when it comes to that subject. I'm a gorgeous woman who happens to be working for an agency that sees being in a relationship as a step up. At least, that's the impression I'm getting. None of the partners are single. And in the years I've worked there, no one single has been promoted to partner. You do the math.

I make up my mind then and there. This comedy show is exactly the kind of distraction I need right now.

I have to be honest and say that I've never been to the Funny Bone. I'm not one for comedy, I guess. But I don't see the harm in trying out one show. What do I have to lose? At least I can get some drinks, hopefully have some laughs, and maybe, just maybe, at the end of the night, I'll feel good enough to solve this lack of a fiancée problem of mine.

GROWING UP, I knew early on that I liked things regimented. If something didn't go as planned—like waking up early so I wouldn't miss the bus—it threw off my equilibrium for the entire day. My parents said I should be more flexible. Learn to go with the flow.

What I took away from that advice? To have a Plan A, Plan B, Plan C… however many plans it would take for my day to go just right. I call this coming prepared. Others call it being anal. I never liked anal, so let's stick to being prepared.

It's what makes me good at my job. I make sure every aspect of a trip goes exactly the way a client expects it to, all the way down to accounting for the weather conditions on a given day. That's why clients book more trips with me and even recommend me to their friends. That's why I deserve to be partner, dammit.

If only I hadn't opened my big mouth and let an even bigger lie fall out. Why the hell did I get myself into this situation? I ask myself this question after each subway stop until I reach the one that will drop me a block away from my destination.

Unfortunately for me, as I climb the steps back to street level, I have no answers. Instead, I get a text from Bob reminding me to submit my fiancée's information by Monday. In the back of my mind, I contemplate not responding, but I also know he knows that I've seen the message. Damn technology and its advances.

I type in a quick reply about confirming the trip with my fiancée. Thank goodness the street crossing sign turns green at the exact moment Bob's reply comes. I plunk my phone into my purse, and for at least a couple of hours, I can pretend the message doesn't exist.

I arrive at the Funny Bone later than expected. The show has already started. A roar of laughter rushes out of the club as if the walls can't quite contain the sound. It's a great energy. One that I really need right now.

I pay the entrance fee and head inside for my complimentary drink. I get two for what I paid, which isn't bad. Had I known that comedy shows come with drinks, I'd have gone to some a long time ago.

I order a martini and drink it while turning to face the stage from the bar. Claire Rox stands at the middle of the stage in all her glory. She wears a leather jacket that's seen better days over a profane shirt and ripped jeans.

She talks casually about how she dated this one girl who got so much Botox that her face couldn't remember how to cry. "Like, literally, her muscles froze," she says. "When we watched a sad movie, tears just leaked out of the side of her eyes." That gets me to laugh. I've seen my share of Botox horror stories.

Then her joke segues into dating this boss woman who insisted on paying for their dinners all the time. That one she turns on its head when she says, "I didn't mind this at first because who wouldn't want free dinners? It was when she said she loved watching me eat that things got weird. Oh the things she asked me to eat while going down on her...."

She flicks a finger for each absurd item she lists, the entire room—including myself—breaking out in uproarious laughter. I laugh so hard I almost spill the rest of my martini.

Her last section of jokes tackles a couple more exes, each more outrageous than the next, my favorite being the one with an online shopping addiction who even shopped in her sleep. I find myself wanting to meet the woman who embodies such sass and confidence. She seems so free with herself, unafraid to share who she is with complete strangers. She's certainly braver than I am.

What is it like to live a life where you don't care what others think about you? What is it like to express your thoughts on a stage where people watch? And what is it like to wear a jacket studded with rhinestone cherries?

Her outfit choice is the most puzzling of all. I would never get caught dead wearing that jacket or the shirt underneath that's giving everyone who sees it the finger. And her boots? I never knew they made snakeskin in neon orange.

I face the bartender and ask, "What time does the show end?"

"Claire is just about to finish. Why?" He eyes me.

I may like girls, but that doesn't mean I don't know how to use my assets to full effect. I lean forward and push my arms closer so that my boobs are crushed together—the mounds play peekaboo at the opening of my shirt. Like any guy, his eyes immediately flick to the creamy puppies barking at him.

"I'm a fan and I just wanted to tell her how much I liked her performance," I say.

Without taking his eyes off my breasts, he says, "Stay at the bar long enough and she'll find her way here."

"Good to know." I nod and end the show for him. "I'll take another martini and a bowl of peanuts."

I don't have to wait long. Claire Rox makes her way to the bar and slips into the empty stool right next to me. I glance sideways and... is that a rhinestone penis, fully erect, on the back of her jacket?

I laugh into my third martini. I have to admit that I might be a little more than tipsy. Whoa! They make them strong at this club.

"What's so funny?" Claire asks, eyeing me up and down.

"You look even better in person," I say, unable to censor myself.

"Sure." She chuckles, taking a sip from her drink. Looks like she's a gin on the rocks girl. "I made a total mess of myself up there."

I shake my head. "Didn't seem like it to me."

"Excuse me... but who are you?"

"Where are my manners?" I reach out. "Dina Oliver."

She wipes her hand over the side of her jeans and takes my hand in hers. "It's nice to meet you, Dina."

I show her the flier. "I saw this and wanted to come to your show."

"Right. Well, if you want an autograph, I can sign it after a couple more of these." She shakes her drink and the ice clinks against the glass.

Actually, I wasn't thinking about getting an autograph, but that's not what I tell her. "That's very nice of you, thank you. I actually just wanted to meet the woman who can live her life so freely. I admire your confidence."

Her eyebrows go up. "Didn't you just catch me bombing up there?"

I shake my head. "Didn't sound like it to me. Anyway, if you really feel bad about it, a good cry helps."

"Hon, I've been doing that for many years and here I still am." She indicates her curves, which I take a moment to appreciate.

"I don't see anything wrong with how you look." Then I amend, "Maybe not the penis on your back. Where did you even find a jacket like that?"

"You like it." She turns around and shows me the penis again. "I found it at a thrift store."

"A thrift... ah, well, okay." I nod. "It does look like it belongs in a store like that."

"I don't know whether I should be insulted or appreciated."

In that moment, I wondered if she is the answer to all my problems.

CHAPTER FOUR

Claire

BEING THE shy kid almost always equated to being embarrassed easily. I usually kept to myself when something happened that wasn't supposed to, because I'd feel my face get all hot and definitely turn bright red like a polished tomato.

Once, I was invited to this party. My first high school party. Even though I was shy, my friends encouraged me to go. They said, "You only live once, Claire." To this day, I don't know why I listened to them. Call it peer pressure.

I went to the party. There was drinking and there was dancing. So that I didn't look like a total loser, I accepted a red Solo cup filled with beer. I told myself I was just going to sip it once in a while, pretending I was drinking when really I wasn't.

But you see, because I'd never drunk beer, a little in my short body went a long way. I was soon tipsy and wandered into the basement, where a game of spin the bottle was in progress. I was surprised when the popular girl in our grade knew my name and asked me to join them. I did.

I sat down between two boys. I didn't think anything about the fact that a girl sat across from me. The popular girl spun the bottle, and beyond all reason, it landed on me and the other girl.

"Kiss! Kiss! Kiss!" they all chanted.

I could feel the heat rise up from my neck to my face. The girl across from me looked uncertain, but she leaned forward as the popular girl urged her. The boy to my right elbowed me, so I leaned forward too.

That was my first ever kiss, and it was with a girl. It shocked me how soft her lips were. What should have been a peck lasted for what seemed like forever.

When I realized the laughing had stopped, I pulled away to see that everyone was staring at the both of us. Unable to process what had just happened, I stood up so fast I grew dizzy. In my disoriented state, what I thought was the door to the outside was actually the door to the garage. I ended up puking against a corner, pressing the open button unintentionally, which lifted the garage doors, exposing my puke-covered front to everyone in the front yard. Not my finest moment.

No more parties for me. And no more alcohol until I was good and ready.

Having someone as beautiful and polished as Dina say that she liked my show when I wasn't even at 100 percent up there tonight was close to as embarrassing as it can get. Tingles run down the back of my neck and my cheeks burn. The bitterness of bile coats my tongue. Suddenly I'm that awkward teen again, puking in front of my peers.

There's something so effervescent about Dina that I can't deny. The way the light plays on her hair. The way she sits with her back straight—posture perfect. Makes me feel like a complete troll compared to her. Yet here she sits, talking to me and making eye contact.

"Don't be so hard on yourself," she says. "I have a feeling everyone had a great time tonight. I know I sure did."

"Oh." I stare at my drink. "That's the one thing you'll learn about comedians—we're never completely satisfied."

"Really? What makes you say that?"

Normally this is where I walk away and call it a night. I don't normally hang out with fans this long. But the longer we talk, the more at ease I am with her. "There's always more that can be done. A bigger audience to play to. Getting the timing of a joke just right."

"It must be so exciting to be up there making people laugh every night."

She's so tall, with striking blue eyes. Never in my wildest dreams have I ever thought of meeting someone like her. She's like a model from a magazine. My collection of exes pale in comparison.

"It's about as exciting as watching your first porn. You don't know quite what to expect, and you find yourself terribly uncomfortable the entire time."

Dina throws her head back and laughs. I sit there, stunned at how captivating the sound is. It's the kind of laugh that I could listen to for as long as it's happening. In fact, I want to keep making her laugh. Is that weird?

"Please," she says after she's regained her composure. "I might have to excuse myself to the ladies' room if this continues."

I wave at the bartender, and he gives me my usual. I look to Dina, and she orders a martini.

"You look like someone who drinks martinis," I say.

"And who is that?" She takes a sip of her drink.

"Someone who's got places to go and things to do. Someone *proper*."

She chuckles again. "My mother will love that you think so. I had to work real damn hard to be the perfect version of myself. Everything needed to be just right."

"Looking at you now? I'd say you've come close."

The softest blush tints her cheeks. "Tell me, Claire, why did you get into comedy?"

"It has nothing to do with natural talent, that's for sure." I grin. "I guess you can say that I kind of fell into it."

"What does 'falling into it' look like?"

Telling someone my comedy origin story comes once in a blue moon. Not many ask, really. So when someone like Dina looks interested, I'm flustered.

I take a couple of fortifying gulps and say, "In college, my friends encouraged me to go up during an open mic at our local bar. I was so nervous I thought I'd pee myself. I don't even remember the first joke I told. I must have blocked out most of that night. But what I do remember is getting that one laugh from a complete stranger. It felt really good to see that someone gets me."

"Now you can make an entire room laugh."

"What about you? What do you do?"

"I'm a travel agent," she says, casually tracing circles around the rim of her martini glass.

Her fingers are so long and well-manicured in a French tip. The more I look at her, the more I'm convinced she's a figment of my imagination. She has to be too perfect to be true. Like Nicole Kidman. I'm convinced that woman is part Fae.

"I thought they didn't have travel agents anymore."

"You would think that with the advent of the internet, but there's still a few of us out there. We're like unicorns. You think we're mythical until you actually see one."

Nice, witty, and smart. The triple threat and my personal brand of kryptonite. I swallow. "What does a travel agent do actually? Asking for a friend." I grin over the rim of my glass as I take a sip.

She mirrors my smile and says, "Let's say you want to book a tour for you and your girlfriend—"

"But that's a hypothetical, since I'm currently single," I interrupt.

"Okay, so you want to book a romantic trip. You can do it on your own, yes, but why go through the hassle of searching each and every promo out there when you can give me a call, tell me what you want, and I'll take care of everything for you? I might even be able to find a deal that you didn't know about that would get you perks you never expected."

"Wow! Sold. Book me that trip."

Again, she chuckles. "I am good at what I do." Then her face falls just as fast.

I lean forward. "What is it? What's the matter?"

"You see, I have this opportunity at my job to finally be the one who travels instead of the one who puts together the travel packages."

"That's great!" I say, but when her expression doesn't change, I add, "Isn't that supposed to be a great thing? I would think that's a dream, right?"

She nods. "It really is my dream, except that for me to actually get the opportunity, I need to take my fiancée with me."

My stomach drops. Just my luck. The woman I think I'm falling in love with on the spot is taken. Why does this always happen to me?

"I still don't see the problem," I say, because I'm a glutton for punishment.

After letting out a huff, she says, "The problem is I don't have a fiancée."

"Oh." All the hope in me that was dashed suddenly puts itself back together again. "Can you just ask someone to pretend to be your fiancée?"

There's a pause. Then she looks me in the eyes and asks, "Will you pretend to be my fiancée so that I can travel the world? You get to travel with me."

"Woah!" I lean back, not sure if she's kidding or actually serious. And I'm the one who tells jokes for a living. "That's a lot to ask for someone you just met."

Her face falls again. "I know. It's crazy." Then she eyes me once more. "What about you? What's the ultimate dream?"

The question distracts me from her request enough that I say, "Getting into the Edinburgh Comedy Festival."

"That's coming up soon," she says, getting a faraway look on her face.

"Yeah, but it's no use." My rejection comes back and stabs me in the heart. It's why I'm off my game tonight. "I have to wait until next year to try again. Maybe I'll have to audition for that acting thing in LA instead." Oh God, I really don't want to audition for that acting thing.

"But you can't give up on your dream!" she insists, eyes wild

"I think you've had one too many martinis." I wave at the bartender. "Bring us something greasy, will you? Soak up some of that alcohol."

"I'm serious." She smacks the bar. "I might know someone who can get you in."

"In where?" I ask, unsure what she's talking about.

"Into the festival this year. I've booked many packages to Scotland." She points that manicured finger at herself. "I have many, many contacts."

"Really?" I ask, studying her as if she's someone about to invite me into a cult. The scary thing is? A part of me might actually believe everything she's saying. That's the drink. The other part, still sober, stays cautious. "You can really get me in?"

"Yes, of course." She smiles. "If this means you'll play my fiancée for this trip I'm going on."

And there it is. The big huge *but* in this entire scenario. "I should have known this was too good to be true."

"Look at it this way. You get to help me fulfill my dream of traveling and potentially making partner at my agency, and I get to help you be a part of the comedy festival." Then her eyes grow wide once more. "You can even use me as part of your act in the future. Once we've appropriately broken up, of course."

"Me? Pretend to be your fiancée...." I shake my head, actually considering it. "How do I know you're not lying to me about getting into the festival?"

She takes out her phone, sticks out her tongue at the side of her mouth, and attempts to dial a number. At her third attempt, I take the phone from her and ask what the number is. She rattles it out just as the bartender places a plate of mozzarella sticks in front of us.

I place the receiver to my ear. "It's ringing."

"Give it." She opens and closes her hand at me, and I hand over her phone. Then she places it at her ear and starts speaking. "Malcolm, it's Dina. It's not too late there, is it? *Oh*, I know you don't sleep. Anyway, I have a favor to ask. I know this hot comedian I think will be perfect for the festival. Can you slide her in?" Dina waits a beat, listening. All I hear is a man's voice that sounds more like a garbage disposal than actual human speech. Then Dina says, "Of course. I can certainly do that for you."

The wait makes my head spin. "What's even happening right now?"

She hangs up and says, "If you agree to pretend to be my fiancée, then the slot is all yours."

I sit there with my mouth hanging open. My brain short-circuits. Then a spark.

"You said I can use this as part of my act in the future?"

She nods, taking a bite of mozzarella. "Only after we break up."

"Is this really happening?"

Dina reaches out and pinches my arm.

"Ow! What was that for?"

"Claire Rox, will you be my fake fiancée?"

What else is there to say but "When do we leave?"

Her eyes brighten as she munches on a cheese stick. "Friday next week. Let's exchange numbers and I'll send you all the details. I assume you have a passport."

"This goes without asking, but are you a serial killer?" I ask, half serious.

"No," she says, just as seriously.

"That's what a serial killer would say."

CHAPTER FIVE

Dina

FOR A job well done, I spend the weekend pampering myself. I take my commission from the European tour and book a full day at the spa. Treatments galore, from a Himalayan salt scrub massage to an Egyptian mud bath. They primp, pluck, and pamper my body until my skin glows.

Then I book a hair appointment with one of the most expensive stylists in the city and ask for a look suitable for someone spending a week at an extravagant French chateau. This includes a trim, highlights, conditioning that leaves my hair soft, and the best Moroccan oil. I walk out of that salon with a strut in my step.

I cap the weekend with Sunday brunch at Balthazar Restaurant, a classic French brasserie in SoHo. Its atmosphere paints the scene of a bustling railway station that hearkens back to the early twentieth century, complete with red banquettes, world-weary mirrors with wine selections printed on them, and a scarred wood bar. I order the warm goat cheese and caramelized onion tart, their smoked salmon with crème fraiche over toasted brioche, and poached eggs with spinach, artichoke hearts, béchamel sauce, and an exquisite aged Parmesan.

To say I feast makes it an understatement. I pretty much taste France on each plate. And in a week's time, I'll actually be there, eating real French cuisine and enjoying the French countryside. My heart tumbles with excitement.

Come Monday morning, I'm floating into the office. Claire texted me all her information the night before. I grab a French vanilla latte from our coffee station and boot up my computer, a bright smile on my face the entire time.

Claire and I have already made plans during the week for travel prep. She promised I could visit her apartment and help her pick out appropriate outfits for the trip. Considering what she wore when we met, I fear the prospect of combing through her closet. I'm hoping her ensemble was only for the stage and not her everyday attire. Even so, I make a mental note to take her shopping in case her wardrobe proves inadequate.

I'm in the middle of encoding all of Claire's passport details when one of my colleagues saunters my way. I glance up a moment and smile at Jade, who was hired a year after I arrived at the agency. Today, her normally pin-straight hair cascades in waves over her shoulder. She's as stylish and chic as I aim to be on a daily basis and just as good at the job as I am.

"I heard you're going on the couples retreat this year," she says, wiggling her perfectly arched eyebrows.

I hit Send and look up at her with a sweet smile. "Just submitted all the information for the trip."

Her jaw drops. "I'm so envious right now, you don't even know. France is like my dream destination."

"It's like all our dream destinations," I say. "Well, maybe except Matthew. He's more like a traipsing around Asia kind of guy."

Jade splays her hands on my desk and leans forward. "Is it true that you have a fiancée? How come I'm only hearing about this now?"

Cue blush. Not because I'm all lovey-dovey, but that's certainly how she takes it. The blush is more for the reminder that this is all smoke and mirrors on my part, and if Jade knew the truth, she'd definitely hate my guts. Heck, I'd hate my guts too.

"It's new," I add to the lie, which is almost not a lie at all. "And you know how I like to keep my private life and professional life separate."

"What private life?" she jokes. "We're all like an open book here."

"Well, there are some chapters that I don't share until they are worth sharing."

Her eyes grow bright. "I heard the couples' retreat is where they discuss who gets to be the new partner."

My fingers tingle, but I play things cool by taking a sip of my latte. "Oh?"

"Don't 'oh' me." Jade pokes at my arm. "You being asked to go is like the anointing. You're a shoo-in for partner."

This time, when I feel my cheeks grow hot, it's for a whole different reason. I speak in a conspiratorial manner when I say, "Let's not jinx it. For all I know, I'm there to act as gofer for the partners the entire trip."

We share a giggle.

Jade straightens and shakes her head. "Either way, congratulations on being part of the trip. The others are too intimidated to say it, but we're all proud of you."

I beam, even though in the back of my mind, my lie haunts me like the ghost of Christmas past. Then I remind myself anyone in that bullpen would do the same thing just to make partner. At least, that's what I'd like to think.

Not five minutes after Jade leaves, Bob makes his way toward my desk from the conference room where he's been with the partners all morning for the weekly Monday meeting. I pretend to be busy with sorting paperwork when really I'm trying to tamp down on the excitement running up and down my back.

As soon as he pauses in front of me, I turn up my smile to eleven and say, "I just sent over Claire's information. When I get confirmation, I'll let you know."

"Well," he says, breathing out. "Someone's had their coffee this morning. Remind me again, who's Claire?"

Taken aback, I blink at him for several seconds before my brain finally catches up. Of course he doesn't know, because I never gave a name for my fake fiancée. Only because at the time, I still didn't have one. Now that I do, names can be used instead of generic nouns.

"My fiancée," I say, gentle in my delivery. "She's as excited to go on the trip as I am."

"Ah, right." Bob nods as if it's all coming back to him now. "I'm certainly looking forward to meeting Claire. Parker hasn't stopped talking about you coming along since I mentioned it to him."

Parker is Bob's husband. When he's not going from country to country modeling or walking the runways, he's hosting all the agency events. The office hasn't had a Christmas party or company picnic that Parker didn't have a hand in.

"Well, you can tell him Claire is happy to meet the both of you."

"Good." Bob pauses, thinking something over. Then he opens his mouth as if he's about to say something. I wait. And wait. But nothing comes.

"Is there anything else?" I prod.

Bob takes a deep breath, then lets it out slowly. "Nothing. It's just a Monday."

Right as he says that, my landline rings. I point at it before reaching for the headset. Bob nods, then saunters away.

I pick up the phone on what I'm sure is only the third ring. The man on the other line is irate at having to wait so long. Bob's words about it being a Monday come back to me. He's totally right, but short of an asteroid barreling into Earth, nothing can sour my mood.

I calm the man down by offering to upgrade his flight from business class to first at no extra charge. That gets him to change his tune right quick.

As I'm booking his hotel accommodations for a trip with his wife to Mykonos, Bob's weirdness from earlier niggles at me. He wanted to tell me something but thought the better of it. I could see it on his face.

CHAPTER SIX

Claire

I WAKE up to a text on my phone. It's still too early in the day for my brain to function properly after the night I've had. Sure, the show went well. But I have to be honest with myself. When I was on that stage last night, my heart wasn't in it for some reason. I think it was an off night. I'm allowed those.

My phone won't stop beeping. I should really change my incoming message tone. It's annoying as fuck when you're still pretty much supposed to be dead to the world.

Without opening my eyes, I roll over in order to kill my phone. Where the hell is that infernal thing? I reach out toward where I believe my bedside table is and start feeling around for the rectangular device.

After a few failed efforts, I finally feel the smooth screen. As if I hit the jackpot, it pings again with another message. Who's been sending me texts this early? Anyone who knows me understands I'm not a fully functioning human being before 10 a.m.

I peek out of one eye and read the screen. As soon as my brain understands the letters spell out Dina's name, it's as if all the blood in my body is activated. I sit up so fast I would have fallen out of bed if I wasn't in the middle of the mattress.

While I rub a hand down my face to wake me further, I unlock the screen and tap on the message app. It opens. Then I tap on Dina's messages. She's sent me five in the span of two minutes.

She's already told her boss. That's good. He's happy to meet us at the airport on Friday. Dina's taken the day off to head over and assess my clothing situation for the trip.

Clearly, she has much to learn about me. I don't pack for a trip until a few hours before I have to leave. And even then, I just dump what I can grab into my suitcase and buy whatever I might need when I land wherever I'm going.

Without thinking, I send her a reply making a joke about not wearing anything that might offend her boss. I get a laughing emoji in return. It makes me smile because I can hear her laughing from all the way over here.

She's so excited about this. Then I send her a congratulations, because it's the right thing to do after someone tells you they are going after the promotion they've always wanted. It's the nice thing to do.

Since I'm already awake, I perform my morning routine. I have a couple of jokes I want to write down. But first I go to the bathroom.

After I wash my face with cold water, Dina's last text finally dawns on me. She's on her way over to my apartment. Like. Right now.

I run out of the bathroom and assess the situation. Old take-out boxes litter the center island of my kitchen. Pizza boxes cover every inch of my coffee table. Clothes litter the floor, creating breadcrumbs that follow the path I took when taking them off. By the window of the fire escape sits a dead plant I don't even remember getting. Might have been a gift from an ex?

My phone pings again. I look at the message. Dina just got off the subway and is a couple of blocks away. My heart pumps like it's full of espresso.

"Shit. Shit. *Shit.*" My dump of an apartment isn't exactly the impression I want her to have of me.

I grab the first thing I can think of: an extra-large trash bag. Once I've shaken the bag open, I use my arm to plow the take-out boxes into the abyss. I don't even care if there's still food in the boxes.

Then I hurry to the coffee table and do the same thing. In my hurry, I might have stuffed one of my coffee table books in with the pizza boxes. The bag sure seems heavier because of it.

I tie off the bag, rush out of the apartment, and drop it in the trash chute.

Out of breath, I return to my apartment, bend down, and pick up each and every piece of clothing on the floor. Having not mastered the art of the hamper, I run to my closet with the intention of stuffing everything in there. Then I remember that Dina's going to look through my clothes. My selections are embarrassing enough without adding dirty laundry.

I jump and sprint and run in circles, trying to figure out where to temporarily hide the armful I'm carrying. Desperately running out of time, I spot the dead plant again. I leap to the window with the fire escape and chuck all my clothes out there, along with the plant.

"Claire?" I hear Dina's voice from down the hallway.

I tug the blinds down and turn around just in time to see Dina standing outside my front door. "Hey!" I greet overenthusiastically as a way to hide my panting breaths.

Her stunning features form a skeptical mask. "Why do you have your door open?"

In five strides, I'm standing in front of her, leaning against the door. "Just threw out the trash. You know, morning routine."

Dina gives me a once-over and grimaces. "Did I wake you? I didn't mean to disturb, but…."

I look down at myself in a ratty T-shirt and joggers whose elastic around the ankles and waist have long since given up. Compared to Dina, in her dove gray V-neck sweater and mint green pants, I must look like a trash person.

Scratching the back of my head, I say, "Just starting my day, that's all." I step out of the way. "Come inside. Do you want something to drink?"

"This is your apartment?" Dina asks. The skepticism in her voice is unmistakable.

"Yup," I say simply.

"It's so… cozy."

Why do I get the feeling she meant to use a different word? "It's not Shangri La, but it does the trick."

She waves her hands, embarrassment coloring her cheeks. "I'm sorry. That's not what I meant. I like it."

Needing something to do with my hands, I say, "I can brew us up some coffee."

"Where's your room?"

"Why do you want to see my room?" A tiny bit of dread falls like a stone in my stomach. The complete seriousness in Dina's tone makes me nervous.

She crosses her arms and gives me the same assessing glance she treated me to when we first met. Granted, she was buzzed then. In the sober light of day, that glance seems to see right through me. Like I might as well be naked in front of her.

"I guess you can say I'm on an exploratory mission." She raises a hand. "Now, before you say anything, I'm here as a friend looking out for your best interests. There are many events to attend during this trip, and I want to make sure—"

"You want to see if I have things to wear for all of them," I interrupt, remembering the rhinestone penis on my jacket last Friday.

"You're getting it." She smiles, breaking down my walls. "I just want to make sure you're prepared for anything. Will you let me help you, Claire? I promise, I come in peace." She touches the center of her chest with one hand and raises the other as if she's about to recite the Pledge of Allegiance.

All the blood rushes from my face to settle at the pads of my feet. Compared to what's probably in Dina's closet, mine might as well be a trash can. "No, thanks. I think I'll shield you from my closet. There are just some things you can't unsee."

Gasping in horror, she asks, "That bad?"

I nod once.

Dina closes her eyes for a moment and breathes in deeply. When she looks at me again, she lifts her chin. "I think I can handle it."

Admiring her bravery, I sigh and gesture for her to follow me.

"It really can't be that bad, can it?"

"Don't say I didn't warn you."

I can almost hear her pause when I lead the way down the hall and push the door open and step aside so she can enter. From my bedspread to my walls, my room is a riot of color. I take a moment to straighten my sheets and fluff my pillows. Then my eyes fall to the floor and spot an older pair of panties—holes and all. I kick them under my bed before turning around.

Dina stops at the threshold. It's obvious from her expression that she wanted to hold in the gasp that escaped her mouth but was unable to stop herself in time. Poor lady looks pale for a second before she steels herself by squaring her shoulders. She marches straight for my closet.

"I call it living in ordered chaos," I tease because I can't help myself.

"I like the paint samples on the wall," she says as she pulls open the doors and assesses the clothing inside.

I drop to my bed and shrug, letting her do her thing as she pulls out a white crocheted dress I found at the same flea market my couch came from.

"They're free. Thought I'd make a collage out of them," I say about the paint samples. I created a sort of gradation from light to dark along one side of the wall. It had taken several trips to the hardware store to complete.

Dina returns the dress and pulls out another one with a huge picture of a cat on the front. "And where would you wear something like this?"

The shock in her question breaks my carefully constructed mask of indifference. I laugh so hard I almost fall off my bed for the second time that morning.

"You think this is funny?"

Only the genuine concern behind her annoyance makes me settle down. "Sorry. Sorry."

She scowls at me before glancing back and dropping the dress she was holding with a yelp. "Oh God!" She turns away from my closet completely, her face a scrunched-up mess.

"What?" I shoot up and grab her arms, all humor gone. "You didn't see a mouse in there, did you?"

"Worse!" She stares into my eyes. "Polyester."

I drop my arms to my sides and sigh, shoulders slumping in defeat. This is just ridiculous at this point. "I know you're only trying to help, but I think it's pretty clear that I have nothing in there that will pass. I think I have a fifty lying around somewhere. We can go to the thrift store—"

Dina shakes her head, shooting down the idea faster than a sniper. "For the events ahead? A thrift store isn't going to cut it."

I look her straight in the face and say, "If you want me to go on this trip, I'm only buying things from a thrift store."

"You have to let me shop for you. I can make a call to my sales rep at Nordstrom. She'll be waiting for us when we get there."

"No." I back away. "Absolutely not."

"Please don't tell me this is about the money."

"It's about the principle of the thing." I cross my arms in defiance. "I only shop secondhand. It's a personal belief of mine, and if you can't accept that, then there's no point in this between us continuing."

"Claire"—she places her hands on her hips—"I get it. You don't take handouts. But you also need to understand that you committed yourself to helping me."

I lift my chin. "I can just as easily back out of that commitment."

Dina takes my hands in hers, giving them a reassuring squeeze. "Then you need to let me dress you."

"Dina—"

"Please, Claire. It hurts less if you stop struggling. Trust me."

"Only at a thrift store," I say adamantly, even as I feel myself giving in.

"We'll start there."

CHAPTER SEVEN

Dina

AFTER A quick grab and go at Starbucks, Claire leads me to the best thrift store in the city. It also happens to be the biggest. According to Claire, going here instead of visiting each and every small one will save us time. I still have my doubts, which is why I have Sara—my personal shopper at Nordstrom—on standby in case we come up short.

Anyway, this is more a lesson than an actual shopping trip, like a makeover for Claire, so I'm hoping I can convince her that buying brand-new clothing isn't all bad. There are sustainable brands out there. My plan is to listen and pay attention, not to actually buy more than what's needed.

Window-shopping. Yeah. That sounds right.

No matter what, I won't allow Claire to buy anything unfit for France. Maybe some dresses and a new pair of jeans. Even a cropped pant, maybe. Well, *new* is a relative term considering the store we are about to enter.

Yeah, that seems doable, I think as we cross onto the street where a huge squat brick building sits.

"The Mustard Seed," I say, looking up at the vintage sign. "How quaint."

"This is where I found the white crochet dress," Claire says, reaching for the door handle.

"I'm afraid to even ask what else is in there if that was the best you could come up with."

Claire grins. "Maybe I'm just fashion illiterate."

"You poor thing." I tug her into a hug, stroking the back of her head. "I'm here to help." Before she can comment, I hold her at arm's length. "First thing you need to know when shopping, thrift or otherwise, is your size."

"Of course I know my size." At the arch of my eyebrow, she says, "I'm a 14 up top and a 16 at the bottom."

The admission makes both my eyebrows rise. "Oh Claire, you are not a 16."

"Uhm, I think I would know my own size. I've been dressing myself since I was six."

A stare accompanies the long pause that follows her statement until I finally say, "You don't honestly believe you're a 14/16."

She backs out of my arms and stretches out the T-shirt she wears that bears the words *I'm a Barbie Girl* in pink glitter scrawled across the chest. "This is a 14. My jeans are a 16."

I touch my cheek and sigh. "I just thought you liked wearing baggy clothes." Then I move my hand from my cheek to Claire's shoulder. "Consider yourself helped. We aren't going home until you know better."

"That's what I was afraid of," she grumbles under her breath.

I consider her for a long moment and then say, "At best you're a 12 up top and a 14 at the bottom. Maybe smaller depending on the style."

"I am so not a 12," she says, eyes practically bugging out of their sockets.

I nod. "Trust me, you're a 12. I have an eye for sizes. Now, come along."

"12?" She follows after me. "I don't ever remember being that size!"

The bell at the door tinkles as I push into the store. Instantly my nose wrinkles as I get a whiff. Oh God, why can't we be at Nordstrom right now?

The open floor plan is filled from front to back with racks upon racks of clothing. The woman at the cash register greets us and calls Claire by name. Then she begins telling us about the new arrivals that are on display. I'm assuming she means new to the store. Claire thanks her before she returns her attention to me.

"What?" she asks.

I sniff several times, then grimace. "I can never get used to that smell. Musty."

"That's what dead people smell like," she quips, earning a horrified glance from me.

"If it weren't for my mom's penchant for buying vintage, I wouldn't even…." I stop myself when I notice the woman at the register giving me the stink eye. Smiling at her, I move toward the first rack. "Once you know your size, know what you are shopping for."

"I was thinking some shirts?"

"Let's focus on dresses first." I reach for the first dress hanging on the rack and push it until all the other clothes are packed together. Then I begin sliding hangers down the pole one after the other in quick succession. "Since you're on the curvy side, stay away from straight-cut dresses. You might as well wear a pillowcase."

"Straight-cut bad." Claire nods. "Check."

"What do you think of halter dresses? I hear the weather in France is perfect for them this time of year. We can even pair it with a cardigan if it gets chilly."

"I never really think about what I wear, to be honest."

I narrow my eyes at her. "I want you to give me an idea of your likes and dislikes when it comes to clothing. That gives me a place to start."

"Well...." She scratches her head. "Nothing too tight. I prefer comfort over fashion."

"Okay, I understand that." Even if I grow pale at the thought. "Since you have rounder breasts, we'll think of accommodating them in something with more structure."

Looking down at her chest, she grabs her boobs and squeezes. "Thank you. I'm quite proud of them."

"That means a halter will work for you if the fit is right, which brings me to lesson number three: always try on the clothes before buying them." I pull out a white lace dress with a full skirt.

"That's pretty." Claire moves her hands from her chest to reach for the dress.

Instead of giving it to her, I look over the dress.

"Not quite right," I say. "Too busy."

Returning the dress to the rack, I move on to the next one. Claire follows, giving the white dress one last mournful glance.

"Stay away from too many patterns. Since you're just starting out, stick with the basics. Easier to build a closet around a few key pieces like an LBD."

"Little black dress," she chirps, happy to know what the acronym stands for. At least she's not completely hopeless in that department. I can work with that.

"Gold star." I pat her head. Then I point at the opposite rack. "Start looking through that side and pulling dresses you might like. Remember your size and body shape. Then we'll meet at the fitting room."

Fifteen minutes later, Claire is behind the curtain of the fitting room with several choices we've come up with. I stay right outside, shifting from foot to foot, waiting with bated breath. If I'm being honest, we actually found a couple of things. I might have sold this whole thrifting thing short.

"Does it fit?" I ask.

Claire pulls the curtain aside. She's in a navy eyelet dress. She spreads the skirt and swishes from side to side. It fits perfectly and is totally cute on her.

"Good?" she asks, a shyness in her eyes.

"Better than expected." I clap once in approval.

Claire pouts, but her doubt quickly disappears when I smile widely at her. Then I point at several other pieces of clothing we picked out. She grabs the green wrap dress at the top of the pile and marches back into the stall.

For what seems like hours, I make her try on dress after dress. My patience never wanes. I give her advice and explain why one style works better than the other, flatters her body more. Every time Claire steps out, I either give her a thumbs-up or down, helping her gauge whether to keep or discard something.

Once she's modeled every item of clothing I deem appropriate, we assess what we've come up with. There are three piles in all, but what holds us up is the Maybe pile, since it's twice as large as the Discard and Take piles. To speed things along, Claire hands all decision-making over to me. With the precision of a chef's knife, I whittle down the choices to ten total.

What should have made things easier backfires on me as Claire points at the entire wardrobe. "I'm not buying all of that."

"But you tried them all on."

"Just to show you that I'm game, but I'm not buying all that."

"Of course not." I come to her side. "I'm buying them for you."

"Oh no, you're not!"

"Claire." I sigh, then murmur, "I thought this was going to be easier."

"Excuse me?"

Louder, I say, "Each dress is less than ten dollars. I'm not breaking the bank here."

"Still." She faces me, crossing her arms, prepared to argue until I see reason. "I don't need all that."

I place my hands on my hips. "You will. There are so many events during our trip that jeans and a T-shirt won't cut it. You might even have to change more than once throughout the course of the day."

Claire tilts her head, considering. "One dress."

"Ten."

"Three. Plus some dressy pants and shirts."

"Five dresses, plus the pants and shirts. We can ditch the orange one."

"I like that one!" Claire doesn't care that her voice rises in the mostly empty store. "Five dresses, including the orange one."

"Thank you for coming," the woman who greeted us earlier says, catching both our attentions. I grin at her. We had a chance to speak while Claire was changing. In her hands are two shopping bags.

"Where are the clothes?" Claire blurts out.

She shrugs. "While you were arguing, I already rang everything up as per Dina's instructions."

"What!" Claire pulls at her hair. "You didn't need to do that."

A wide grin stretches across my lips as I take the bags from her and say, "Lunch is on me."

"We are not in a movie," Claire says, shaking her head in disbelief.

Chapter Eight

Claire

I SHOVE my hands into the pockets of my jacket as my short legs make quick work of the pavement beneath me. Dina carries the shopping bags filled with clothes that never in a million years would I have picked for myself. Sure, there are a couple of dresses in there that I like, but are they me? I'm not completely sold on the idea.

As I lead the way to the Greasy Spoon for a late lunch, Dina babbles on about how fruitful the shopping trip was.

"If I'm being honest, I was ready to pull you out of there and drag you all the way to Nordstrom," she says, not at all out of breath. She hasn't stopped talking since we left the Mustard Seed.

"See? Thrift stores aren't that bad," I respond over my shoulder in an offhand manner.

My mind swirls with doubt and anxiety. Never a good combination. Not once did Dina let me make my own decision when it came to picking out my clothes. In the end, I gave up since it seemed like the easy way out of the uncomfortable hell I found myself in.

"We actually found a couple items that completely surprised me," she continues, totally not picking up on my tone. "Now, would I make it a practice to shop at a thrift store? Not really."

That comment grates on my nerves. I turn around so fast that Dina barely stops in time to avoid slamming into me. She looks me up and down.

"What?"

"I don't think this is a good idea," I finally say. There's still time to back out of this thing.

Dina tilts her head. "I don't understand. What's not a good idea? The clothes? Because I honestly think you look good in all of them."

I roll my eyes and remind myself that I'm a grown woman and grown women shouldn't stomp their feet like young children denied cotton candy at the fair. "Were you even going to let me pick my own stuff?"

Taken aback, she leans away from me and blinks. "What? Of course, of course."

"You know, when people repeat themselves that's a sure sign they're lying."

"That's not true. Not true—" She sucks her lips in.

"Ha!" I point at her face. "See, you were just about to repeat yourself."

"I don't see the problem here," she counters, lifting the bags in her hands. "You approved the clothes before I paid for them."

"No! You paid for them without my say-so yet."

"I figured I'd be the one more qualified at this."

"And what makes you say that?"

"Have you been to France? Have you ever stayed in a chateau?"

I don't have to think twice. "No."

"Well…." She pauses. "Neither have I, but I've planned trips like this for myself many a time. I've planned down to what I will wear. So I know what we need for our trip."

"There's no 'our trip.'" I turn around and keep walking. I'm hungry and won't have the strength to continue this argument until I get something to eat.

I push my way through the glass swing door of the Greasy Spoon and spot an empty booth. Dina hurries close behind me. I make a beeline for the vinyl bench and slide inside. Dina pushes the bags onto the opposite bench before sliding in too.

"Are you sure about this?" Dina asks. "You're sacrificing Edinburgh because I bought you clothes?"

"Can we pause until the food arrives?" I ask, satisfied with my form of revenge. "I'm starving."

Dina gasps. "We're eating here? I know a quaint café not too far from here."

"You're doing it again," I say as I look through the menu.

"What can I get you ladies today?" one of the servers asks as she stops at our table.

"I'll have a stack of buttermilk pancakes with a side of bacon and a giant chocolate milkshake." I look toward Dina, who can't quite keep her aghast expression from slipping out. "What do you want?"

Dina glances at the menu, then pushes it aside until she realizes it's actually the paper place mat the diner uses. She pulls it back toward herself and sighs. She makes eye contact with our server.

"Hello, Charmaine," she says in the sweetest voice. "I'll have a cup of coffee, black."

"That all?" Charmaine asks, totally charmed.

"I'll let you know if I want anything else."

Charmaine's pencil scribbles on the menu and she walks away.

It doesn't take five seconds until Dina starts in on me again. "Look, all I wanted was to help you find the right clothing to wear. I don't see what's wrong with that."

"Want to bet that before we leave here Charmaine slips you her number?" I ask, wiggling my eyebrows.

"What?" Dina's jaw drops. Then she lets out a *pshaw*. "She's not going to do that. And don't think that this will distract me from you wanting to duck out of this trip because I bought you clothes."

I lean against the booth's backrest. "This is going to be a thing with you, isn't it?"

"Can you please just say what you mean so I don't have to keep guessing?"

"You needing to control things," I say. "You must have your way or nothing else."

"Buying you clothes is not me wanting to have my way. I just don't want you to embarrass yourself at the chateau."

"Hon, I think you're forgetting that I'm a comedian. I embarrass myself for a living."

Her shoulders drop. "That's not…. You know what, have it your way. Bring whatever clothes you want."

I'm about to respond when Charmaine returns with our food. Technically, my food and Dina's coffee. Without even hiding it, Charmaine slips a paper toward Dina.

"I get off at six," she says before walking away.

I laugh around the chunk of pancake stuffing my mouth.

Dina unfolds the piece of paper. The mortification on her face is priceless. During this shopping trip alone, I already have a ton of material I can use to build a new act.

Then the thought hits me.

Maybe I'm being too hasty about this whole backing out of the trip thing. Maybe I should see where this goes. So Dina bought me some clothes.

I swallow down my pride along with a healthy bite of bacon. The salty sweetness mingles with the bitterness of letting someone control my choices in clothing. That's not so bad, right? I can get through this. At least, I hope I can.

"Will you stop laughing at me?" Dina asks, cheeks pink.

I cover my mouth and swallow before saying, "Who knew you would be such a chick magnet?"

She grows serious, setting her coffee aside. "The trip."

"Don't worry your skinny little ass about it," I say even if there's nothing skinny or little about Dina's ass. Charmaine was right to slip Dina her number. I'm sitting across from a gorgeous woman. "What time do we leave for the airport?"

CHAPTER NINE

Dina

COME FRIDAY morning, I wake up in an excellent mood. Finally, I've made it to the end of the week. The day we fly out. I give myself a congratulatory stretch by raising both my hands over my head and wiggling my toes.

Then I lie there for a little while longer. I recall sitting by the bar as Claire performed her set last night. She was magnificent on stage despite what she said about fighting a case of nerves five minutes before the show. I honestly couldn't tell. Maybe it's different for performers.

I've never laughed that hard in my entire life. I won't admit this to anyone even if you put a gun to my head, but I almost peed myself. That's how funny Claire was. Having her as my pretend fiancée might actually be so much fun.

Afterward, we went back to her apartment and I helped her pack. She marveled at my expert folding skills. I didn't even want to know what she did when packing for an out-of-town gig before I came along.

Unable to stay in bed any longer, I push aside my sheets and sit up. Then I swing my legs over the edge of the bed. I roll my head from side to side to clear the crick in my neck.

I shrug on my silk robe and make my way to the bathroom, where I conduct my morning ablutions. Afterward, I splash cold water on my face. As I dab the water away with a soft towel, I look at my reflection.

No bags. No puffiness around my eyes. No signs of how sleep-deprived I've been these past few days preparing for the trip. What wonders a good night's sleep can do.

Last night when Claire and I got to talking a little more, I discovered that she was the headliner, as she called it. The main act, she explained when I asked what being a headliner meant. It's thrilling to know that I know someone with star potential.

She was so popular that almost everyone at the club wanted her autograph. I knew she'd kill it at Edinburgh. This is the first time that

I'm actually happy I used my connections to help someone out. If there is someone who deserves to make it in her chosen field, it's Claire. Especially after putting up with me all week.

Before we parted last night, I told her I would pick her up so we can go to the airport together. I told Bob that everything was set, and he looked forward to finally meeting my fiancée. My stomach tumbles at the thought. I say a quick prayer that everything goes well—for the both of us.

I check the weather, and it's a beautiful spring day in the Loire Valley. According to the travel liaison of Chateau Blanc, the second week of May, which is our stay duration, is the perfect time, since we're facing milder weather. Smaller crowds so we get the town practically to ourselves. The wine tasting is what I'm looking forward to the most.

I go to my kitchen and stand in front of my expensive, top-of-the-line espresso machine. I figured if I was going to pretend to be a traveler to Italy, I might as well have the tools to make the best espresso. Now I can actually taste real espresso in actual Italy one day. I'm so excited I almost spill the coffee beans as I place them in the machine.

I press Start and the beans are ground up and spit out as fine powder into the portafilter. Once it's full to the brim, I pack it in before I place it into the group head. Then I place my cup directly below it and press the shot button.

In seconds, the machine drips out the perfect little espresso shot. While it's still hot, I bring it to my lips and take a sip. I enjoy the heavenly taste of the medium blend that I favor, and it wakes me up further.

I toast some bread, spread butter over it, and enjoy my simple breakfast standing up in my elegantly appointed kitchen. I spent years getting the look of my apartment just right. I picked out all the furniture to give me a feel of the places I wanted to go.

My kitchen represents Italy. My bedroom represents Greece. My living room is Spain. My mini balcony is France. And my bathroom is England.

My closet, in which I spend about fifteen minutes second-guessing my choice of outfit, is New York all the way. I pull out a sheath dress the color of plums and pair it with nude pumps. Simple. Sophisticated. Representative of the jet-setting woman I am about to become. I even put on large sunglasses as if the glare of the sun off the Mediterranean is in my eyes.

My phone pings, followed by a skip of my heart. I pick it up expecting a text from Claire. Instead, I get a notification that my town car is here.

So I pull up the handle of my rollaway suitcase, pick up my purse, and bid goodbye to my apartment for the week. The driver opens the door for me, and I leave him my luggage to place in the trunk. When we're on our way, I give him Claire's address.

After thirty minutes, we arrive at Claire's apartment building. She's already waiting outside in a red leather jacket—which I'm starting to think she has a penchant for. She pairs this with sensible flats, the skinny jeans I picked out at the Mustard Seed, and a shirt with huge lips across her chest. My lips tighten into a smile. At least the shirt doesn't have holes in it.

I would have preferred the sundress I left out for her last night. I rub my hands over my lap and take a deep breath. What she's wearing is fine. It's comfortable. It's fine, I repeat for good measure.

I widen my smile as she hands over the bags to the driver. It's a total bonus that I met a great girl. It seems to me that Claire isn't the lonely type, so I have to make sure to guard my heart from getting too attached. I don't want to end up falling in love with her during all this only to find out that she doesn't feel the same way at the end. I'd like to avoid the heartbreak as much as possible. We're in this as friends, nothing more.

She gets in and flashes me her own smile. "Good morning."

"Hey," I say, suddenly hyperaware of how good she smells. A mix of musk and floral scents.

Obviously Claire has a life of her own. A career that she's worked hard to get. Once this is over, we will go our separate ways without anyone the wiser.

I'm just totally grateful that she agreed to this.

"Got your passport?" I ask, reverting to my travel agent mode.

She pats her breast pocket. "Right here. Got all our travel documents?"

The smirk that comes is one of challenge. "You mock me. I'm offended that you have to ask."

"Well, you said you'd take care of everything. I'm just making sure that nothing is missing." She wiggles her eyebrows. "I'd hate to get stopped at the terminal just because our travel documents are lacking."

"Dagger to the heart." I place a dramatic hand to my chest. "Is this what I have to look forward to from my fiancée on this trip?"

"Speaking of which"—Claire gets serious all of a sudden—"maybe we should get our stories straight. We didn't get to talk about our backstory all week. In case we get questions, you know? When and where did we meet?"

I settle into my seat and get ready to ace this crash course on our fake relationship while heading to the airport.

"That's simple," I say. "Let's stick to the truth. We met at a comedy club. A couple of years ago. We hit it off right away, and the rest is history."

She nods. "I like that. Okay, who proposed? Because someone always asks, and they will surely want the story, so we need one, too."

"Good call. In the movies, it always comes up." I have to think about it. "How about you proposed? You seem like more of the romantic type than I am."

"And you're assuming this based on?"

I bite the inside of my cheek to keep from grinning at her raised eyebrow. "Well, I'm just hedging my bets since my coworkers don't see me as the type who will propose."

"Okay, I look forward to unpacking why in the next few days that we're together." She rubs her chin while I take a deep breath to resettle the flutters in my stomach her words caused. "If I proposed, it's at Serendipity over their frozen hot chocolate. Oh crap!"

"What?"

"What about the ring? You're not wearing a ring."

My eyes immediately drop to my fingers and the lack of accessory there. "Uhm… what if we say you're waiting to get the ring from your grandmother?"

She frowns. "But my grandmother is dead."

I sigh. "Claire, this is a fake engagement. You don't have to actually get me a real ring."

"Oh, right!"

We share a laugh. Yet at the back of my mind, something pinches. I ignore it as we continue to exchange more details about ourselves in case anyone asks. Where did we go on our first date? Where did we first kiss? What happened during meet-the-parents?

We go with the simplest of answers. I met Claire's parents over Thanksgiving, and she met mine over Christmas. Cliché, I know, but we don't exactly have time to concoct a better story. Anyway, what matters is how believable our performance is.

By the time we arrive at the airport and the car rolls to a smooth stop at our airline check-in, a woman in the navy-blue uniform of Air France waits for us. The driver places our luggage in the cart while I give our names to the woman. She says she will take care of our check-in and that we can proceed to the first-class lounge, where we can wait until boarding.

"First class?" Claire asks in surprise. "Swanky. I've always been an economy girl when I have to travel for shows."

"It's all paid for by our host, Chateau Blanc. It's part of the experience. This means the clients can book a package that already includes airfare and transfers to and from the airport," I say with a casual air in my tone, but really I'm super excited.

"Dina!" Bob's voice reverberates from the first-class lounge.

I suck in a breath. For a moment I forgot that he and the other partners would also be there. At first I'm frozen in my tracks, not knowing how to react or even how to move. Then warmth engulfs my hand. I look down to see Claire entwine her fingers with mine.

"You ready?" she whispers from the side of her mouth as she winks at me.

Our eyes lock. A momentary thrill runs through me. So it begins. I smile back and nod.

CHAPTER TEN

Claire

WHAT THE hell am I thinking? I grab Dina's hand the second I notice her freeze in her tracks. I suspect the man wearing the white linen suit must be her boss, if her reaction is any indication.

Since deciding that I'm giving this arrangement a chance after our shopping trip where she bulldozed all my choices, I really want to make this work. I think of my career. I think of the new act that can come out of this experience. I think of my future.

Not to mention that she looks so good in that dress. It hugs all her curves, the fabric molding to her body. She looks like an A-lister from the tip of her head to the pointed toes of her shoes. My heart leaped at seeing her when she picked me up.

We didn't really have time to discuss the contact situation in the car. I make a mental note of that for when we're alone again. For now I'm holding her warm, soft hand, wondering if the rest of her is just as soft, about to meet her boss.

"This must be Claire." The man who must be Bob approaches with a welcoming smile.

He has salt-and-pepper hair, combed back, giving him that dignified look most men can only dream of having. Close behind him follows a man about ten years younger with sandy blond hair and the kind of tan you only see in LA. He reminds me of my Ken doll. I was never much for Barbie. Ironic considering my current status in life.

"And you must be Bob," I say, reaching out with my other hand and shaking his.

I make sure my grip is firm. My dad always says you can tell a lot about someone by the way they shake hands. Bob's is just as firm.

"Dina told me a lot about you," I add, recalling as much as I can from our conversation in the car.

"Nothing bad, I hope," Bob says before he gestures to the man beside him. "This is my husband, Parker."

"Nice to meet you, Parker," I say, taking his hand in mine as well.

He blushes. "You're Claire Rox. When Bob told me that you're Dina's fiancée, I couldn't believe it. I'm a huge fan. I never laughed so hard in my life."

"Maybe you'd do us the honor of performing for us during our stay at Chateau Blanc," Bob says.

"Oh, I don't think that's appropriate," Dina says right as I open my mouth. "We're working and Claire is on vacation, so—"

"I can do a little set, hon," I say, cutting her off. The heat in the sidelong glance she gives me singes my eyebrows and turns me on. "I never say no to performing."

"Wonderful," Bob says. "I'll see what I can do when we get to the chateau. Dina is right, though. It might look like we're on vacation, but we're actually working." He winks.

Normally when guys wink, I get this creepy vibe from them. Usually it's because they think they can turn me from liking girls. Those guys are assholes who see lesbians as challenges instead of actual human beings who would never be attracted to *them* even if we did date guys in general.

But Bob? His wink is more good-natured.

He waves us over so I can meet the other partners. I don't let go of Dina's hand the entire time. It's more for my sake now than hers, since I'm nervous. I shouldn't be, really. I've been through so many meet-and-greets that I'm an actual pro at it, but this is my first time pretending to be someone I'm not. My guard is up.

There are three other partners and their spouses. Their names fly over my head as soon as I finish meeting one couple and move on to the next. I'm hoping that the more I interact with them during this trip, the more I'll get used to knowing their names.

As we're about to board, my phone rings.

"Hey, Dwight," I say. "Can you give me a sec?"

I cover the receiver and whisper to Dina, who's looking at me with concern, "It's my agent. You go on ahead."

Her eyebrows come together. "You're not standing me up, are you?"

I flash back to our argument at the diner. I can understand why she feels standoffish. I shake my head. "I'm already here, aren't I?" I ask. "Have a little faith."

She gives me a once-over, like she's trying to make up her mind if she can trust me or not. Since I'm wearing something other than the dress she picked out last night? I get it. I'd like to at least pick my own clothing, thank you very much. When she doesn't move, I practically roll my eyes at her. I have a feeling I'm going to have to do a lot of reassurance this week to get her to trust that I'm in this.

When she finally turns around and follows the flight attendant sent to escort those in the first-class lounge to the plane, I return my attention to Dwight.

"Hello?" I ask, seeing if he's still there.

"Made up your mind?" he asks back.

"Actually, about that—"

"This is a huge opportunity for you, Claire. We're talking sitcom," he says, cutting me off as if he already knows what I'm about to say. "If this takes off, you could be set."

"I understand." I nod as if he can see me.

"Then why aren't I hearing a 'Book my flight to LA, Dwight' from you?"

"That's because I'm performing at Edinburgh."

"I'm sorry, I didn't hear that correctly. Did you just say you're going to perform at Edinburgh? As in the comedy festival happening in a few days? That Edinburgh?"

"Yeah." I stuff my free hand into the pocket of my jeans. "I met someone who can get me in. That's where I'm headed now. Well, France first."

"What?" I've never heard Dwight sound more confused than he does in this moment. "What's in France?"

"An opportunity. Anyway, can you draft a press release? I'll send you over the details when I have them."

"Claire—"

I hang up the phone, not waiting for what else he has to say. I'm scared that if I tell him what I'm doing to get the Edinburgh spot, he'll find a way to convince me not to go through with it. Dina doesn't trust me already as it is, based on the look she gave me.

The flight attendant gives the final call for boarding first class. I raise my hand at her like a grade-schooler showing her teacher she's present. She waves me over and I go on and follow.

CHAPTER ELEVEN

Dina

WATCHING CLAIRE enjoy first class is a treat I never expected. It eclipses the nerves brewing in my belly, taking my mind off the fact that this is my first time on a plane. Her beaming face when she got into her pod drove away all my fears. I'm a traveler now—I should start getting used to being on planes.

While Claire marvels at the plush blanket, the free headphones, the complimentary snacks, and the pod that reclines all the way into a bed, I settle in for the almost-eight-hour flight. This is an average when flying out of JFK to CDG. Some flights can take as long as twelve hours depending on any stopovers and the wait time.

Chateau Blanc is really pulling out the stops. The partners at our agency are the only ones occupying the entire first-class floor. I get the feeling this is part of the package that they want us to sell to travelers. Not that you get the entire floor to yourself, but that you get a curated experience and going first class is the start of that experience. I can already imagine spouses-to-be wanting this destination honeymoon.

A stern flight attendant walks around balancing a tray of champagne. She bends down ever so slightly toward me and offers a glass. I take one, because how can I describe what will happen on the trip if I don't partake of all that it offers?

"Look, there's a strawberry in the glass," Claire says, pointing at the bottom of the champagne flute.

I lean over and whisper at her, "For a celebrity, you sure are surprised by the more luxurious things in life."

She almost chokes on her drink. "I don't know what you've heard, but comedians, especially ones like myself who're still climbing the ranks, don't make very much. I usually fly economy, remember? The fanciest hotel I've stayed at is a Best Western."

Her response surprises me. I would have thought, with the packed house and the full-on audience laughter every night I've come to see her perform, that Claire is making bank. Maybe she really does need Edinburgh to agree to being my fake fiancée for a week.

"But Edinburgh will change that?" I ask, making sure my voice doesn't carry over to the other partners, especially Bob and Parker.

She grins and wiggles her eyebrows at me. "That's the plan."

I honestly don't know how to take her response. I should be happy that she's pursuing her dream. I pushed her to it. But a part of me can't help but feel slightly used. Then again, isn't that what I'm doing too?

Claire puts on her headphones and plays a movie as soon as we're up in the air. I, on the other hand, open a magazine. The trashier the better.

Soon enough, we land in Paris at a couple hours after lunch. We are escorted from the plane to a line of Bentleys waiting curbside—one for each partner. The attendants trolleying our luggage around hand the carts over to our waiting drivers.

In a move that I don't expect, Claire opens the door for me. I'm taken aback by the chivalry for a second before I slide in and make room for her. She scooches to my side and closes the door after her.

"How long until the chateau?" Claire asks, adjusting herself in the seat then buckling in.

I pick up the information packet wedged into the side of the seat. The front shows a beautiful sprawling estate surrounded by greenery. The Loire River runs alongside it, giving the grounds a lushness. I flip open the folder and read through the welcome letter.

"It's even customized with our names," I say, handing it over to Claire.

"And the paper feels heavy." She balances the letter in her hands.

"What does that have to do with it?"

"The heavier the paper, the fancier the place."

"Point taken." I raise my eyebrow at her simple yet true observation. "It says here that it will be a two-hour drive, so we will get there late afternoon if the traffic permits."

"There's even a schedule of events." Claire looks over at the packet, leaning toward me.

Her proximity brings me into the orbit of her perfume once more. I take a deep breath of it and remind myself to ask her what it's called and where I can buy it. At the same time, I'm struck by her warmth. It's a comfortable air that surrounds her that I don't mind being in.

"Seven-course dinner," she says. "That's fancy, isn't it?"

I nod, momentarily lost in her scent. "Means we'll have to dress up. That little black dress I packed will be perfect."

"Good to know."

"Why do I get the feeling you're not going to wear it?" I narrow my eyes at her.

"What makes you say that?" She plays off my scrutiny by looking through the list of activities.

"Oh, maybe because right now you're not wearing what I picked out for you?"

She huffs, then asks back, "Are we going to argue about this after that fantastic plane ride?"

I consider her question. As much as my need to make sure everything is just right begs for me to release the kraken, Bob and Parker didn't seem to mind what Claire is wearing when they met. None of the other partners commented either. In fact, they all seemed to like her. Were charmed even.

I tamp down on my emotions and breathe out my initial rising annoyance. "You're lucky you made such a great impression back at the airport, or we'd definitely be having this fight."

Grinning with satisfaction, she says, "Now, I think we need to talk about something important that we forgot to discuss when you picked me up this morning."

Closing the packet, I shift sideways so I can look at her. "What did you want to talk about?"

"The PDA situation."

At first I wonder what she means, since we haven't really done anything yet. Then I recall her holding my hand out of the blue when Bob approached us. It touches me that she's considerate enough to want to discuss it.

"I'd say holding hands is a good start," I tell her, my neck growing hot, but I refuse to adjust the collar of my dress.

"What about kissing?"

I don't know how to respond to that. I'm not sure if she's being serious. But the more I stare at her face and the lack of humor there, the more I'm convinced that she's really thought this through.

"I don't think we'd be required to kiss," I say, trying to play off the conversation as unimportant.

"But just in case? I don't want to overstep my boundaries with you." She squeezes the back of her neck. "I mean, I feel like I already invaded your personal space by holding your hand without your permission earlier."

The warmth in my neck climbs up to my cheeks. "I feel like you did that to save me."

"Does that mean if kissing you will save you then you give me permission?" This time there's an unmistakable glint of mischief in her gaze.

I roll my eyes and breathe out again, this time to dispel the unruly butterflies in my stomach. "Yes. If you think kissing me will save me from something, then by all means go on ahead."

"Good to know." She wiggles in her seat more as if to resettle her butt farther in. "Man, these cars are totally the bomb, aren't they? I may get used to this."

"I think that's the point."

CHAPTER TWELVE

Claire

MY JAW pretty much unhinged itself the second we drove into the town of Montsoreau. It felt like stepping into an older world, one preserved from the ravages of convenience and technology. The quiet town with its stone buildings stretched along the Loire River.

Then our driver told us that to get to Chateau Blanc, we needed to drive along the river with its water like glass, reflecting the late afternoon sky. *Gorgeous* seems like too tame a word to describe what I'm seeing.

The picture of the chateau on the folder Dina showed me when we left the airport couldn't compare to the grandeur of the place the Bentley floated into. This thing is a freaking castle. The grounds are expansive. Shit, I feel like I stumbled onto the set of *Downton Abbey* or something.

Cherry trees dot the landscape. Bushes with pink flowers line the driveway, the gravel crunching beneath the car's tires. I'm so excited that even the bursts of green that should have calmed me don't.

"They really should redo that packet thing," I say, unable to keep my eyes away from the building we're nearing with its many large windows, white stone walls, numerous chimneys, massive balconies, and turrets. Like actual freaking turrets.

"Why do you say that?" Dina asks, looking from the front of the folder to the place. Or should I say, *palace*?

"The real thing is way better than that picture." I point at the front of the folder.

She sighs like I do when a large slice of decadent chocolate cake is laid in front of me. I forget everything but the sinful dessert and the goodness about to settle on my tongue. It's a point between desire and ecstasy.

"You're right," she finally says, swooning. "This place is absolutely magical and totally romantic. I'm already composing my spiel in my head for prospective couples who will honeymoon or vacation here."

"If the outside is like this? I can't wait to see the inside," I say as the car rounds the massive fountain with its lovers in tight embraces as water washes over them, and continues toward the entrance. The carved marble couples in various states of undress seem way too erotic for the front of what is essentially a hotel. But then I remember that I'm in France.

A line of staff waits at the ready. Bob's car is the first to stop and he's the first to get out. Appropriate since he's the big man. He moves toward another man in a very expensive suit and they shake hands. This guy must be the big man of the place. I know the type. I've met many a club owner with the same vibe.

Once all the cars stop, the staff spring into action. Doors are opened, luggage is whisked away, and welcome drinks are served. Crisp white wine for the weary travelers.

"We should really pace ourselves with the booze," I say, not wanting to embarrass Dina with my drunk self. She's not pretty.

"Oh, but this vintage is absolutely delicious," she says after taking a sip. She looks at the glass and stares at the golden liquid inside.

The big man Bob shook hands with calls for our attention in French-accented English that sounds so sexy. I can just imagine a woman sounding that way. I would be completely powerless to say no—to anything.

"Welcome to Chateau Blanc," he says from the top of the entrance steps. "We believe that we have created the ultimate romantic experience for couples, which is why we have invited you to see for yourselves, and maybe fall in love all over again after this week is done."

I eye each of the couples clutching each other close. Parker looks just about to faint. Dina and I stand close, but not close enough like the others. I'm afraid to make a big move because I don't want to startle her. Instead, I sidle closer so we keep up appearances. She doesn't move away, so I take that as a sign that what I'm doing is okay.

"Your luggage has already been brought to your rooms," the big man says. "Please take a moment to relax and change for tonight. Dinner starts promptly at seven."

A woman in a tight dress and equally tight bun approaches us. "Madame Oliver and Madame Rox?"

"Yes." Dina speaks for the both of us.

"My name is Pullen. I will be escorting you to your room." She gestures for us to follow her.

"What kind of a name is Pullen?" I whisper as Dina and I trail behind the lady.

"Very French," she whispers back and giggles.

We climb the steps and enter a dramatic lobby with ornate metalwork, walnut paneling, stylized light fixtures, a grand staircase, and marble walls and floors. My eyes don't know where to look first. My head feels like it's on a swivel.

Pullen talks about the place. When it was built. Who first stayed here. Why it was converted into the resort it is today. I only pay half a mind, taking in all the grand furniture, the textured wallpaper, and the paintings of couples in different romantic situations.

In the back of my mind, I go to naughty places. I wouldn't be surprised if orgies happen after hours at this place. Maybe it's on some secret itinerary we haven't been shown just yet. Some *Eyes Wide Shut* kind of deal.

We're taken to the third floor, down the hall, to a corner room with double doors. If you thought I wasn't impressed yet, well, I can't be any more impressed than I am now. For me, as long as the sheets are clean and the bathroom is tidy, I'm good.

Pullen opens both doors and gestures for us to enter. That we do. She reminds us of the time we have to come down for dinner and that if we need anything, we should just call down to the concierge.

When my jaw drops this time around, I distinctly hear a pop. Seriously, I think it's dislocated at this point. The one-bedroom suite has a huge balcony that looks out over the river. The living room has two—count them, two—couches made from a fabric that's so expensive I'm afraid to touch it. The coffee table might actually be gold-plated, and the flowers on top are totally fresh sitting in their crystal vase. A mix of roses, lilies, and hydrangeas. There's a desk at the corner filled with stationary, postcards, and fountain pens. In the other corner sits a round dining table for two, but considering how lovely this place is, I don't know why you'd want to eat cooped up in your room.

I wander into the bathroom and my eyes practically pop out of my head. "That's one hugeass tub," I say.

The double vanity isn't too shabby either. And the closet? It's totally bigger than the one at my apartment.

"Oh dear," Dina says from another part of the room.

"What's the matter?" I ask, leaving the bathroom.

I go in search of her and find her in the bedroom. My feet halt right at the entrance as I take everything in. There are rose petals scattered all over the bed in the shape of a heart. There is a welcome basket filled with chocolates, a bottle of champagne, and… is that a bottle of lube? Among other naughty things. I knew it! Definitely orgies after dark around here.

"They gave us the honeymoon suite." Dina shakes her head while rubbing her forehead. "I think maybe this is because we're the only ones not married."

Hiking a thumb over my shoulder, I say, "I can totally sleep on the couch. I have two to choose from."

"Why would you do that?" Dina looks at me like I just told her I could fly. Then she points at the bed. "That's definitely a king. We can take one side each and not even touch if we don't want to."

"Are you sure?" I ask, swallowing, suddenly feeling very hot. "I really don't mind—"

"Stop it, Claire," she interrupts me. "I don't want you looking like you didn't sleep well. We're sharing the bed, end of discussion."

"End of discussion," I say.

"Why don't we unpack and start getting ready for dinner?" She smiles. "From the way they keep repeating that they start at seven promptly, I get the feeling they'll start without us."

I give her a grin. "And we wouldn't want to miss that. Why don't you take the shower first and I'll clear the bed of all this?"

"You're a lifesaver."

As soon as Dina enters the bathroom and closes the door behind her, I lift my suitcase onto the bed and unzip it. The clothes she packed are still there, but I smile at the new additions I snuck in after she left. Dina neglected performance outfits. I need options for Edinburgh.

I remove each article of clothing and hang them up on my side of the closet. Assuming there is my side and her side, as Dina has yet to unpack anything. Note to self, Dina likes things neat. Must not mess things up. I'll surely try. I make sure everything is neatly put away. Sweaters, T-shirts, and a pair of pj's go into drawers, along with underwear good for a week.

On the nightstand, there's card that lists all the complimentary services included with the stay. I smile at the free laundry. Good to know. If I run out of clothing by some miracle, at least the hotel can clean them for me. The dirty underwear situation makes me think twice, though, since I'm uncomfortable having a stranger handle my bras and panties. Those I'll just wash myself in the sink. Maybe. We're not there yet.

I'm in the middle of rummaging through the gift basket when Dina exits the bathroom with her hair wrapped in a towel and the hotel robe covering everything else. A slight blush goes over me at the thought of her being naked under all that plush terry cloth. Right at that moment, my hand pulls out a pink vibrator.

Dina tilts her head. "They really rolled out the red carpet for us."

I look down at my hand and drop the vibrator. "Yeah…. Huh… don't know what to do with that."

She grins at my discomfort. "I'm sure you do." Then she hikes a thumb over her shoulder. "Bathroom's free. I suggest you get going, because I don't want us to be late."

Face smoldering, barely able to look her way—my hand still feeling the vibrator in it—I grab the dress and underwear I'll be wearing and shuffle past her. I immediately close the door behind me as soon as I walk into the bathroom. I take a deep breath of the steamy air and cover my mouth, stifling a laugh that's bubbling out. Could have been worse.

I turn around. My eyes pop wide open. Despite the shower door and floor being wet, the bathroom doesn't look like it was used.

Once I've removed my clothes and placed them in the second empty hamper—the first already has Dina's travel clothes in it—I move to the shower and reach for the knob that should open the tap. Nothing's there. Only a touch screen panel.

"Oh-kay." I fumble around. My fingers search for the right button.

The shower turns on, but glacial waters flow out. I let out a yelp, which prompts me to bring my hands to my mouth. No. I'm not going to call for help. I can do this.

I hug the wall farthest from the spray and look at the panel again. This time I study the icons. The shape of flames with a plus and minus sign beside it can't be more obvious. I tap the plus while I place my other hand underneath the waterfall. I release a sigh of relief when the water finally reaches the temperature I prefer.

I don't know how long I spend, only that Dina calls from outside the bathroom and reminds me to get dressed. As much as I hate leaving the heavenly shower with multiple jets—which I discovered while lathering my body with soap—I hit the power button and open the glass door.

I grab a towel from a stack and start drying off. Once I'm done, I wrap my head with the towel and begin slapping on the most heavenly-smelling lotion. Not small bottles either. These are full luxury bottles. I'm impressed.

Relaxed and totally grinning, I face the dress that Dina picked out for me at the Mustard Seed. I tilt my head. It didn't look small when I tried it on.

I unzip the back and begin shimmying into it. As is my custom when buying thrifted items, I wash them first before wearing. I pull the zip up and run into my first problem. The zipper gets stuck.

"Shit," I whisper between my teeth.

I remember this dress being easy to close when I tried it on at the store. Oh crap. Did it shrink in the wash?

Gritting my teeth, I take a huge breath in and pull the zipper up with all my might. I manage to get it all the way up this time. But the second I exhale, I hear an audible rip.

CHAPTER THIRTEEN

Dina

I STEP out of the bedroom wearing my favorite little black dress and heels to find that Claire is still in the bathroom. Checking the time on my phone, I realize we're running late. Not that getting from our room to the restaurant will take more than five minutes, but still. I refuse to be late to this dinner.

"Claire, you got to get a move on," I call out, not wanting to peek into the bathroom and interrupt her privacy. Don't get me wrong. I'm tempted to peek in, I'm just not going to.

"Go on ahead," she answers. "I'll be right there. Save me a seat."

"I don't need to. They'll seat us together, most likely."

"All the better. Just give me a couple more minutes. I may have to move into this bathroom."

I chuckle as I make my way to the door. Pullen gave us each a key card. I make sure mine is in my clutch before walking another step. It's there, along with a tube of lipstick and a twenty. Euro, that is. You never know when you'll need the money, my mom always says, which is why I had mine exchanged at this place I know back home that gives the best rates. Then I pull out the shopping bag I hid in the front closet while Claire stepped into the bathroom and bring it with me.

Ready for what I assume will be an amazing dinner, I leave our room and make my way to the stairs. Descending the steps isn't easy in heels, by the way—I wobble a couple of times because of the plush carpets. Already I'm feeling the decadence of the place. The ambiance really does lend to romance. The perfect honeymoon destination.

The luxurious décor extends into the restaurant. Crisp white linen covers the tables. The place settings all match. The tapers all stand at the same length. I'm totally feeling myself right this moment.

Bob catches my eye and waves me over. The flutters return to my stomach, but this time I don't freeze in place. Looks like Claire and I will be dining with him and Parker.

"Looking dapper, gentlemen," I say, appreciating both men in their suits and ties.

The dinner didn't specify black tie, so it's not as fancy as gowns and tuxes, but it's still a sports jacket kind of deal. I make a note of that since it's something worth mentioning when pitching the Chateau Blanc to couples.

Bob stands and pulls out my chair for me. "Where's Claire?"

"She's running a little late," I say. "That bathroom really got to her."

"Isn't it divine?" Parker says. "I can live in that tub."

"Funny. Claire feels the same way," I tell him.

"How's the honeymoon suite treating you?" Bob asks as he returns to his seat.

"It's lovely," I say. What I don't say is that if only Claire and I weren't faking being in a relationship, it would be damn fantastic.

"Looks like we're not the only travel agency here," I say as my eyes travel the room.

"I say bring on the competition." Bob nods. "The more the merrier."

I'm inclined to agree. Knowing that other people will be pitching the same place only makes me want to do a better job at booking couples here. I haven't talked to Bob about the commission on this place, but from the looks of things? It's pretty high.

The dinner starts, and I have no idea where Claire is. I don't know if she's coming. I don't know if she drowned in that tub. All I know is that I'm left here sitting alone with my boss and his partner.

In the back of my mind, I remain hopeful. I refuse to believe that Claire would stand me up. She agreed to help me. She wouldn't leave me hanging like this. She didn't strike me as that cruel of a person. And it doesn't look like she's still holding our little shopping trip over me.

Have I become a joke to her? A punch line she can't wait to deliver at one of her shows? Well, it's not even funny and I'm not laughing.

"She told me she'd be right out of the shower before I left the room," I say as I bring up my wineglass for the third time.

"These appetizers are amazing," Parker says in order to change the subject.

"I wonder who their chef is." I echo his positive tone as best I can.

Bob glances at the menu that lists all the courses coming out tonight. He keeps a neutral expression, but I know he's annoyed. I push my panic down as far as it will go so that it doesn't show on the surface.

I'm forced to entertain the possibility that Claire might not come. What will happen to me? Surely Bob won't fire me for something like that. Will he suspect that I'm making this all up as I go?

I'm slowly dying inside with each minute that passes. There are worse things than being out of a job tomorrow. One, I may never be unchained from my desk ever again. Two, I will certainly never be considered for an opportunity like this ever again. Three, Bob will be so disappointed in me, I may never be able to prove myself for as long as I work at his agency. The last one makes my gut twist the most.

Each reality is worse than the next. All because I trusted someone I just met. That will teach me to put too much stock in a stranger.

At least I know where to find her. I take solace in that fact because I'm already crafting what I will say to her when I hunt her down. It's so unfair that she put me in this situation.

My heart breaks slowly, piece by piece. I can barely hold the tears back. I blink as a way to hide them, but I can see Parker looking at me as if he understands something about me that even I don't.

Then, just when I'm about to lose all hope, I look up and spot a sparkling riot of color bouncing behind the hostess. The light in the restaurant catches each and every sequin sewn into the gaudiest jumpsuit I've ever seen. Instant mortification swallows me whole as I recognize Claire approaching.

A part of me wishes she had stood me up instead. Has she even thought to run a comb through her hair? Strands are flying everywhere.

Is it too late to shoo her away? Or maybe the ground will part beneath me and swallow me whole. If I thought I was dying inside earlier... well, I'm completely deceased now from total embarrassment.

As the hostess stops near our table, I plaster a smile on my face and stand. I approach Claire and give her a small kiss on the cheek. This is so that I can whisper-hiss into her ear.

"First, where have you been? It doesn't take that long to get ready and to get here," I say under my breath in an annoyed tone.

"I'm so sorry," Claire says, giving me a hug. "I ran into a little hiccup."

I try not to stiffen as I return the hug, but I still say, "Second, what the hell are you wearing? I don't remember adding that into the suitcase when I packed for you last night."

"Not the time to scold me for my choices. Your boss is watching."

Instead of giving her an answer, I turn around and return to a happy smile and say, "Better late than never."

"I love what you're wearing," Parker says in surprise and awe.

Bob stands up and pulls back Claire's chair like he did for me earlier. "Glad you could finally join us."

Parker beams. "I was just telling Bob about your performance at the Laugh Factory. I laughed so hard that by the end of your show I had abs."

"That's what I like to hear," she says, giving Parker a brilliant smile. "That's why I have to ask for your forgiveness. I totally fell asleep in that tub. Must be the jet lag."

"It happens," I say, taking my own seat. "You should have taken that nap on the plane like I told you."

"I should have, but I was too busy watching all of those complimentary movies."

Bob chuckles. "I get all my movie viewing on planes too."

Claire runs her fingers through her hair. "Again, I have to ask for your forgiveness. I didn't think the hostess was going to let me in for being tardy."

"That's all right," Bob says, laughing that deep belly laugh of his. "You can make it up to us by performing tonight. I already told the host."

"Oh, Bob, I don't think—"

"I have a good twenty minutes in me," Claire interrupts, taking my hand and giving it a squeeze. "I'm already in my performing jumpsuit."

It takes everything in my power not to melt upon contact. I have to remind myself that I still haven't forgiven her for her outfit of choice tonight. But she came. That's more than I hoped for when I was panicking.

"You should see the outfits she wears on stage, hon," Parker says, a light in his eyes that I haven't seen until now. He's completely starstruck. "They are absolutely—"

"Horrible? Gaudy? Outlandish?" Claire asks, cutting him off.

Parker laughs. "I was going to say charming. Your sense of style complements your act."

"He should know," I say. "Parker is a model."

Claire's eyebrows shoot up. "I should have known that kind of handsome makes money."

They all laugh—even me. I can't help it. When Claire is on her A game, she's absolute fire. I appreciate every second of it, because from the look of things, Bob is completely taken with her.

"Then it's a good thing that I get to see part of your show tonight," Bob says.

"I'm usually at the Funny Bone, but I can give you and Parker tickets to any of my shows," Claire offers.

"Actually," I chime in, "Claire is going to perform at the Edinburgh Comedy Festival on Wednesday."

"Really?" Parker clasps his hands together in adoration. "That festival is absolutely massive. Are you going to perform your Fat, Fun, and Single set there?"

Claire nods before she takes a sip from the wineglass the server has just filled in front of her. "That's the plan. It's a great stepping-stone for my career. I'm absolutely terrified."

"I get the fun part." Bob gestures at her clothes. "But I don't understand the single part."

"You forgot the fat part, but I love you for quietly omitting it."

Again, another round of laughter bursts from the table. We're so loud that the tables near us are turning and looking. Who knew I have a bona fide celebrity sitting beside me? Suddenly I square my shoulders and lift my chin in pride.

A bit of awkward silence follows while we're all waiting for a response that Claire hasn't given yet. She merely says, "I just hadn't updated that part of my act yet. After these shows, I'll move on to a new act with a new tour name."

Bob and Parker nod as if fully understanding what Claire means.

After we finish eating our canapés, servers whisk away the plates and set down the entrée, which is the second course. It's like a well-choreographed dance. The last server says we're about to taste the best salmon mousse in all of France.

The spoonful I take into my mouth melts like the richest butter. The lemon juice compliments the sourness of the cream and the sweetness of the salmon. My eyes practically roll to the back of my head. I can't imagine the meal getting any better, but we still have five courses left.

From the sounds of pleasure coming from everyone at the table, I'm not alone in my assessment of the food.

"Good Lord," Claire says. "Can we all admit that this is better than sex?"

Parker chuckles. "I'm almost right there with you, but Bob's got some skills."

There is a moment of silence. Bob's as red as a beet, and I feel heat climbing up the back of my neck. Then Claire lets out a boisterous laugh so infectious that Bob and Parker soon join in. The cringeworthy pause takes a second to dissipate from my body before I too am laughing with them.

We enjoy each course as they arrive. We go from a seared white sturgeon with caviar beurre blanc to a divine coq au vin to the smoothest lemon sorbet I have ever tasted. My tongue has never been so happy.

All the while, Claire continues to regale us with story after story of her escapades. She's got Bob and Parker eating out of the palm of her hand.

Just before dessert, the host approaches our table and lets us know that the stage is set for Claire. She excuses herself from the table, and I get tingles all over. Watching her perform is a total treat, even if I am a bit nervous about what she'll say.

The stage is actually a platform the staff set up at one side of the restaurant. Claire climbs up without a problem. A spotlight shines on her and she sparkles. Literally.

She starts by greeting everyone with a good evening, then dives right in by asking the question, "What's wrong with farting in elevators?"

Already she's getting laughs. She points at the audience.

"You know who you are. Don't even try to deny it. You've stood at the center of a packed elevator and let one rip."

The level of laughter rises as she turns her attention to a table from a rival agency. They're elbowing this one guy who I assume is guilty of the deed. I grin.

"When did farting become a bad thing?" Claire asks. "I mean, it's a natural bodily function. Not only do people shame you for farting in public by making this face…." She scrunches up her face to demonstrate, and they laugh. "But they will also pretend like they don't fart at all, and walk away judging you."

The audience laughs. I get the feeling she's just warming up. In that moment, fart jokes and all, I've never been more attracted to one person. Claire makes funny look so damn sexy.

"I went to Las Vegas recently," she continues, "and little did I know that men would be hitting on me left and right."

The intro to that joke is met with sexy whistles and jeers. She keeps going.

"Since I'm a proud card-carrying lesbian, I had to think of creative ways to let them down. One time I'm riding the elevator back to my floor when a man gets on from the second floor. When I'm on an elevator, I like standing near the buttons, because I like to be in control like that."

She mimes pushing buttons in such a suggestive manner that I feel my cheeks grow warm. That, of course, gets her laughs as well. I, on the other hand, am feeling other things.

"So this guy comes in, right? And I'm standing by the buttons, and he starts hitting on me. I pretend that I don't hear him. He keeps at it. Do you know what I mean, ladies?"

She gets an agreement from the women in the room.

"Well, here's a way to get a man to stop. I turn around slowly and point to myself and say, 'You can see me?' Not only do you get the man to stop flirting, but you also convince him that the hotel he's staying in is haunted."

All night long, we're laughing too hard. Which is evidently followed by drinking too much. And we end up ordering the most decadent of desserts on top of what we've already eaten.

A beautiful chocolate cake slice is placed in front of Claire when she finally returns to our table.

"That is one gorgeous sight," Claire says. She lets out a hum that borders on erotic.

"Go ahead." I hand her a fork. "You deserve it."

She slides it between us and says, "I can't possibly finish this all. Share it with me?"

The look in her eyes is intimate and filled with longing. Unable to break the act and say no, I pick up the fork. Claire takes a pinch from the cake, as do I, but instead of putting her fork into her mouth, she brings it to my mouth. Her eyes point to my fork, and I bring it toward hers.

Soon there's a flash and Bob says, "This is brilliant. A beautiful shot."

He shows Parker, and the model agrees. "You two make a beautiful couple."

"This is going out to all of our social media accounts." Bob taps the screen of his phone. "It's a great way to show how romantic this trip really is."

As Claire looks at the photo from Bob's phone and asks him to send it to her, I start to wonder what exactly I have gotten myself into. This is going out to the public. I like Claire. I really do. But I get the sense that my life is about to change in ways I'm not prepared for.

CHAPTER FOURTEEN

Claire

WHEN THE dinner ends, Dina and I move to the chateau bar next door, not ready to call it a night just yet. It's as swanky a place as the restaurant. The leather seats along the bar. The polished hardwood. The plush velvet booths. This place is ripe for getting drunk, loosening up, and possibly getting laid afterward.

"That went well," I say as I lift up onto one of the stools.

"Better than well. I think Bob's in love with you," replies Dina, getting on the stool next to mine.

"I get that all the time. The gays love me." I wave at the bartender and order us drinks.

"What happened to you?" she asks as she throws a cashew into her mouth from the bowl of mixed nuts.

I sigh. No point in lying at this point. "You know the dress I was supposed to wear?"

"The black one?"

Sheepishly, I nod. "Well, it shrank in the wash. When I put it on and managed to zip it up, the fabric in the back ripped."

Her eyes widen a fraction before she says, "I thought you were going to stand me up. See, that's why you don't buy clothes from thrift stores."

"I should have read the care instructions more carefully." I turn to face her. "I'm sorry you worried I wouldn't show. I panicked and didn't know what to do, so I went with my stage outfit instead."

The bartender returns with our drinks. A martini for Dina and a gin on the rocks for me. She thanks the man and takes a sip of her drink.

"Damn, this is good." She smacks her lips together. "But I appreciate the apology. I actually thought my life was over for a second."

I lean forward, brow furrowed. "I shouldn't have tried wearing the dress when I already suspected that it shrank. When we get back to the room, I'll check the rest so that I don't run into the same problems later on. Friends?" I reach out a hand to her.

Instead of taking it, she picks up a shopping bag she's been carrying around and hangs the handles on my fingers. "Here, I bought this for you."

"What's this?" I look into the bag.

"Try it on."

I take out a black jacket that looks pretty expensive. "Gosh, Dina, you already bought me most of what I brought along. This is just too much."

"When I saw it, I thought of you."

My eyebrow arches of its own volition.

She rolls her eyes. "Fine. I bought it to accompany our purchases from the Mustard Seed. Little did I know that you would come in what's tantamount to shiny fish scales."

"I snuck in my stage wear after you finished packing." I chuckle, but I put on the jacket anyway. "This is way too nice of you. Especially after I was late to dinner."

Dina tilts her head, studying me. "It's actually not bad." Then she takes both lapels in her hands and jerks me forward. "But pull something like that on me again and there won't be a place on this earth where you can hide from my wrath. Do we understand each other?"

Terrified and turned on at the same time, I nod. "Look, I'm in this all the way."

"Good." She lets go of the lapels. "Just keep the drinks coming."

"I'll buy you all the drinks you want." I clink my glass with hers.

Dina lets out a long breath. She's practically slumped over. "You don't know what almost seeing your future slip away can do to a person."

"Oh, I'm well aware of that kind of scenario. As a comic, I deal with that kind of rejection a lot."

"Where do you see yourself going with being a comedian?" she asks as our next round of drinks arrives, along with another bowl of mixed nuts.

I take a couple of walnuts and pop them into my mouth. "The main goal is eventually getting to shoot a special. I really want to snag a Netflix deal."

"That's pretty ambitious. I admire that." She takes a sip of her martini and sighs. "These things are always better at bars like this. The vodka they use is top-notch."

"Since we're talking about ambitions, what about you? Is this promotion the dream for you?"

She shakes her head. "The promotion is certainly a stepping-stone. The dream is traveling the world. Day in and day out, I create travel packages for others to enjoy. I want to be able to see the places I've been booking all this time."

"Being on a plane isn't everything it's cracked up to be, you know. I mean, except for being in first class, of course."

"It's not the vehicle that matters, but the journey and the destination. I'd sit on a plane all day if I had to."

"Try saying that when your flight is delayed several hours."

"That's a jaded thing to say." She frowns.

I sip my gin and enjoy the smooth taste that slides down my throat. "I guess it's the comedian in me. I'm on a plane a lot going from one state to the next on weekends."

"That must be so exciting."

"It is. Then it gets the same after a while."

"I hope I don't ever feel that way about travel."

"Where do you get that optimism from and where can I get myself some?"

She chuckles. "I guess I had to learn it for myself. My parents taught me there's nothing that I can't do if I put my mind to it. The positive attitude comes from knowing that if I work hard, I can achieve my goals."

"My parents were the complete opposite. They left me alone for the most part." I stare into the clear liquid in the glass. "At least your parents took an interest in you. It didn't help that I was also painfully shy as a kid."

"And yet you're a comedian who gets up on stage to perform for a lot of people."

I have to laugh at that. "The irony doesn't escape me, believe me. Sometimes I still feel like that shy kid."

"Okay, this conversation is getting deep. Let's do twenty questions. What's your favorite movie?"

"*The Thomas Crown Affair*, the new one. I find Rene Russo really hot. What about you?"

"I love *Shakespeare in Love*. Gwyneth was absolutely gorgeous in that movie. It won her the Oscar, you know."

I didn't know. "Okay, favorite book. Mine is *Born Standing Up* by Steve Martin."

"*The Color Purple* by Alice Walker," she sighs wistfully. "It's a classic lesbian novel."

"Is that the one with Oprah in it?"

"Have you seen the movie?"

"No. I just know that Oprah's in it."

"Favorite food?" Dina asks, doubt starting to color her expression. "Mine happens to be Japanese. I love tempura and donburi bowls."

"Mine is pasta all the way. You don't get this fat without getting a few carbs into you." I wiggle in my seat, trying to lighten the mood.

Dina reaches out and clutches my arm. I turn to look at her. She has a serious expression on her face. "I actually find your curves quite attractive."

I suck in a breath, not having expected those words to come out of her mouth. "You find me attractive?"

"Your curves," she says, letting me go. "I wish I had boobs and an ass like that. Sometimes I think I'm too straight up and down."

"Can we not play the game of who's more insecure? Because it's starting to look like that's the only thing we have in common."

"We don't like the same books or appreciate the same food—so what? That's completely fine. Couples don't always have to like the same things. That would be boring."

"Well, then." I raise my glass to her and joke, "Thank God this is all a scam."

CHAPTER FIFTEEN

Dina

WE STUMBLE back into our room in a fit of giggles well past midnight. Claire takes off her clothes as she goes, kicking off shoes and unzipping zippers. My hands itch as I watch her sway her way into the bedroom.

Not having the strength to ask her to pick up after herself, I bend down and reach for each shoe and the discarded rainbow sequined thing she calls clothing. The shoes go on the shoe rack along with mine, side-by-side like they belong together. The jumpsuit goes into the hamper in the bathroom.

My eyes glide over the state of the place. Not a complete mess, although it still looks like someone used the space. The black dress lies discarded on the floor.

It might be the booze running through my system, might be the jet lag, but pinpricks of sadness stab at my heart when I pick up the dress. Frayed fabric remains where the zipper was attached.

"Poor dress," I say as I fold it like a flag for a fallen comrade. "You did your best."

The scrap goes straight into the trash.

Despite heavy limbs begging for sleep, I take a moment to tidy up. I could have let housekeeping take care of cleaning the bathroom, but my brain won't let me rest if I lie down knowing the lotion bottles aren't aligned perfectly or that the towels aren't stacked neatly.

Once the bathroom is returned to its tidy state, I remove my makeup and brush my teeth. Then I recall I won't be sleeping alone. My stomach tumbles.

I pick up my tinted moisturizer and rub some on until it covers my spots and blemishes. Then I add a light cheek cream for some color. Brush on some mascara for lengthening and fullness. Dab on a plumping gloss. And finish the fresh makeup/no makeup look with the best setting spray in the market. Nothing is budging until I use makeup remover in the morning.

I change into my silk nightgown with a matching robe that I stashed in the bathroom earlier. As a last thing, I tap a drop of perfume on my wrists.

Refreshed, I pad through the suite and enter the bedroom. Claire is on the bed already, with the covers pulled up to her chin. She blinks at me as I move to my side of the bed.

"Are you wearing makeup?" she asks.

I pump lotion onto my hands from the nightstand and start rubbing my palms together. "I don't sleep with makeup on."

The lie comes out easily. No one, and I mean no one, has ever seen me barefaced. Especially someone I'm dating. This may be a fake relationship, but I'm not being caught dead sans makeup. What if we needed to evacuate the hotel for some reason?

"Okay, my turn." Claire pushes away the covers and stands. She's in a T-shirt too many sizes too big, and sweats.

My heart leaps in my throat and beats there for several minutes.

As she uses the bathroom, I distract myself by finishing my unpacking. At least she put away her clothes properly. I try not to focus on what she calls entertainment outfits.

Claire returns minutes later all fresh-faced. I hide a pout.

"Your skin is glowing," I blurt out as I tuck myself in. "You have to share your nighttime routine with me."

"You mean soap and water?" Claire says as she returns to her side and covers herself once again with the comforter. "Are you okay with the temperature? I like my surroundings cold."

I think on it a moment. The bed is plush and slowly acclimating to my body warmth. The comforter isn't too stifling.

"I'm fine," I finally say, resting my head on pillows like clouds.

Claire turns off her bedside lamp, and I do the same. There is a moment of pause. A silence that hangs between us.

I'm all too aware of the other human being lying beside me. That if I reach out, without even needing to stretch that far, I can touch her. What will happen if I do? Will she pull away?

My fingertips sweat at the idea.

"Is this weird?" Claire asks.

My heart jolts. "What's weird?"

"It's been almost a year since I slept with someone else in the same bed," she confesses. "It feels weird."

I stare up at the ceiling and breathe out slowly. She hasn't dated anyone in a year. In the back of my mind, a tiny part of me celebrates. But why? We're here for mutual benefit and nothing more.

The reminder calms my overreacting heart. "Think of it like a slumber party."

"I didn't really have slumber parties."

That makes me want to sit up and face her, but I stay prone. "Surely you had friends."

"I didn't say I was never invited," she clarifies. "It's just I never really went to any. Painfully shy, remember?"

A big part of my chest aches for Claire's younger self. "Well, consider this your very first slumber party."

Claire chuckles.

When a second round of silence comes over us, the air feels less awkward.

EARLY THE next morning, I wake up to Claire's soft snores. She murmurs something that makes me think she's awake. I freeze. Seconds later, she quiets and her breathing returns to the deep steadiness of sleep.

Ever so slowly, I push away the covers and swing my legs over the edge of the bed. Once on my feet, I tiptoe my way to the bathroom, hoping against all hope that the floors don't creak. Chateau Blanc may have been renovated down to its studs, but that doesn't change the fact the building is old. Like centuries old.

Only when I reach the bathroom do I allow myself to feel relieved. I quickly perform my morning ablutions, then head for the sink, where I proceed to wash off all the makeup on my face. When I'm sure that every pore is squeaky clean, I move on to brushing my teeth. Then I run a brush through my hair, making sure no strand is left tangled.

Lastly, I repeat my nightly routine. Tinted moisturizer, some light blush for color, a touch of mascara, but this time I switch to a subtle pink lip gloss.

I give myself a once-over in the mirror. Then I check that nothing in the bathroom is out of place. Satisfied, I make my way back to the bedroom on feet that barely touch the ground.

Inch by careful inch, I get back into bed, lie on my back and fan out my hair, and close my eyes. Minutes later, our room phone rings.

The shrill trilling wakes Claire with a start that ends in a string of choice curse words.

I sit up as if I've only just woken and pick up the phone, which is on my side of the bed. "Hello?"

"Bonjour, Madam," a pleasant feminine voice says. "This is your wake-up call. Breakfast is served at the Premiere Lounge."

"Thank you," I say.

"Pullen has asked me to remind all our guests that the wine tasting starts at 10:30 am."

The call ends and I put down the phone. The hairs at the back of my neck rise. I turn to see Claire watching me with bleary eyes. Her hair is sticking out in many directions, and there is what seems like moisture at the corner of her mouth.

"What?" I ask, unsure if she's annoyed or confused or both.

"You wake up looking like that?" she grumbles, kneading the side of her head.

"Looking like what?" I ask back innocently, unwilling to show the behind the scenes of the production.

Claire rolls her eyes. "I need a couple aspirin."

"I have some in my purse," I say, getting out of bed. "Why don't you go to the bathroom and wash up. I don't want us to miss breakfast."

"What's on the agenda today?" she asks while scratching one asscheek on her way out of the room.

"Wine tasting."

Chapter Sixteen

Claire

At breakfast, the mouthwatering spread before me stays ignored. The pounding in my head rivals that of a busy construction site. My biggest fear in that moment is to pick up a freshly baked croissant, put it in my mouth, chew a couple of times, and heave the remnants of my stomach contents—which is basically acid at this point.

If I remember correctly, Dina drank as much as I did last night. Yet there she sits across from me, looking fresh as a daisy in a summer dress with frills. Damn, she looks gorgeous. I don't know how she managed to wake up all rested and like she's worth a million bucks while I crawled out of bed tasting death in my mouth, drool on my pillow, and with hair like a rat's nest.

Life is just unfair sometimes.

I sigh into my Bloody Mary. The vodka in it gives the tomato juice a sweetness I didn't expect. Quite enjoyable, actually. Each sip brings me a little more back to life.

Dina and Parker babble on about something. I'm so deaf in the ears from all the hammering that I can't tell what they're saying.

Bob leans toward me with sympathy on his handsome features. "Nursing a hangover?"

"Drank too much coupled with a bit of jet lag," I manage to say over the lip of my glass before taking another gigantic swallow.

"Then maybe you should sit this wine tasting out," he suggests.

After being late to dinner last night? Not going to happen. It's because of Dina that I even get a chance to perform at Edinburgh. All she asked is I play the dutiful fiancée. And that's what I'll do.

"I'll be there," I say. Then I pull out the celery stick from my glass and munch on it like a chipmunk finding a hoard of nuts.

Dina glances toward me and smiles. My stomach does a flip. For a second, I think I'm really going to be sick.

When she looks away, the queasiness eases.

AFTER BREAKFAST, we all gather in the lobby, where Pullen meets us. She's in a head-to-toe black outfit that is so French, she even has a beret on.

I look down at the floral dress with a full skirt that reaches my knees and wish I'd worn jeans instead. But Dina made a fuss about the wine tasting being a semiformal event. Apparently it ends with a scrumptious late lunch. Her words.

My only consolation for having to wear a dress is the comfortable flats. Thank goodness too, because according to Pullen, there's some walking to be done to reach Chateau Blanc's vineyard. The best in the Loire Valley. Or so she says.

I for one am not a wine person. In my mind, it's basically grape juice that can get you drunk.

"Excusez-moi, madames et messieurs," Pullen says to catch our attention.

As one, we turn toward her. The eagerness in the room buzzes. Dina mentioned on our way to the lobby that the Loire Valley produces some of the best wines in the world. With this tasting being free, I understand the mounting excitement.

"If you will follow me," Pullen continues, gesturing toward the doors. "We will make our way to the vineyard and to the wine cellar where the tasting will commence."

In groups of four, we make our way out of the chateau into the beautiful morning sun. The weather is mild, with a slight coolness to the air that makes walking comfortable. I'm wearing the jacket Dina gave me. I'm not going to lie, it's the fanciest thing I currently own.

It's about a ten-minute walk down a tree-lined road. The walls of the chateau soon give way to rows and rows of grapevines. We walk along the fields, and I'm continually grateful for the flats I have on. How Dina can walk in heels—albeit wedges—down the sloping hill amazes me.

"To your left are Chenin Blanc," Pullen says with a wave of her arm. "They are what the chateau winery uses to create its sparkling wines and sweet wines. The ones on the vines will not be harvested until November, but Chateau Blanc has a small greenhouse where we grow grapes for guests to taste." A woman in Chateau Blanc colors hands her a basket, which Pullen passes down through the group. "Go ahead and taste for yourselves."

Dina picks out a grape, but instead of putting it into her mouth, she brings it to my lips. On reflex, I lean away and grimace.

"Shouldn't we wash it first?" I ask. "God only knows the kinds of pesticides on that thing."

Smiling, Dina tosses the grape into her mouth. There's an audible pop when she bites down on it. She hums in delight. The sound reaches into me and thrums my insides.

"Looks like someone neglected to read their pamphlet," she teases, taking another grape while walking.

I wince. "I have you for that."

"Well, if you've read the information, you will know that Chateau Blanc only uses the biodynamic method when growing their grapes."

"Meaning…." I let my voice trail off, wanting Dina to finish her explanation. There's something so unbelievably attractive about her when she starts talking shop.

"Meaning they don't use chemicals and they take the words 'all-natural' to a whole new level, to the point where they even track the lunar cycles for the best time to harvest."

"That's some woo-woo shit for wine."

Dina brings a new grape to my mouth, and I gladly take it. We share a blush when my lips accidentally graze her fingertips. She looks away while I'm distracted by the sweetness of the grape that bursts in my mouth.

Pullen leads us toward a pair of wooden doors embedded into what looks like the entrance of a cave. A man wearing a jacket over a suit waits there.

"May I introduce Pierre." Pullen gestures toward him, and he tips his head like he's wearing a top hat. "He is our head sommelier, and he will be taking you through the tasting."

Pullen leaves us in the care of Pierre, who opens the wooden doors and leads us into a cavern with lit sconces embedded directly into the rough stone walls. Barrels lying on their sides line the hall. As we go deeper into the cave, the temperature starts to drop.

"One of the things that make wine from the Loire Valley stand out is our cellars," Pierre says as he continues even deeper into what seems like an infinite tunnel. "We store our wines within the limestone of the valley itself."

I spy Dina shiver, but she has on a brave face. The dress beneath the jacket I'm wearing has sleeves. Hers doesn't.

As the tunnel opens into a massive room filled with shelves upon shelves of wine, I shrug out of my jacket and drape it over Dina's shoulders.

"What about you?" she asks, looking me in the eye while simultaneously hugging the jacket closed.

I grin. "That's what the booze is for, and the extra layer of fat."

She rolls her eyes, but before she can say another word, Pierre is already talking about the wine bottles set out on a center table made of thick wood. He picks up the first bottle and proceeds to uncork it while our group picks up wine bottles to examine. Pierre starts explaining things like tannins and earthy flavors.

The first is one of the sparkling white wines Pullen spoke about earlier. Bubbles float to the surface of the clear golden liquid. Dina is enraptured by the words that come out of Pierre's mouth.

I, on the other hand, drink the entire serving in one gulp. It leaves a tart aftertaste at the back of my throat, and the bubbles tickle my nostrils. My allotted portion isn't enough to chase away the cold within the cellar. I can even see the breaths coming out of everyone.

The next is another white wine, but Pierre says something about it being sweet. I don't care. Once again, I down the entire fourth of a glass he pours me.

Since I'm still slightly drunk from the night before, my second glass of wine reawakens my buzz. The hangover is gone. Now I'm in the floaty warmth. Okay. Feels comfortable now.

After the third glass of white wine, we move on to reds. If I didn't care before about what Pierre was saying, all the more I don't care now. My feet barely feel like they're touching the ground.

By the fifth glass, Dina's trance is finally broken and she turns in my direction. Me? Well, turn on some music, because I want to dance.

"Claire?" She sidles closer, concern deepening the lines on her face. "Your face is all red."

"Really?" A hiccup that faintly tastes like burnt strawberries escapes me. "You're right. This wine's good." Half my words come out as a slur.

"Have you even been wine tasting before?" she asks, pulling me away from the group.

She tugs so hard I almost stumble. Good thing for flats.

"My first time. Why?" I ask back, proud that I still have some of my wits.

"Because you're not supposed to swallow the wine," Dina hisses out. "You're supposed to taste it, then spit it out."

"What?" I grimace. "Where does the spit go?"

She points at the metal vase-looking thing.

"Gross." I feel all the wine I wasn't supposed to swallow start to come up. "I think I'm going to be sick."

"Come on." Dina puts down her glass and takes mine and sets that aside too. "I'm taking you back to the hotel and putting you to bed."

"But the tasting—"

"No more tasting for you," she interrupts.

"Boo!"

She doesn't let me say anything else. Instead, on strong hands, she almost lifts me out of the cave. Or maybe I'm just too drunk to resist.

Chapter Seventeen

Dina

BRUNCH THE next day is a scrumptious thing. Claire practically eats everything on the menu at the chateau restaurant. The ravenous comedian even tries to steal a bite of my quiche, which I valiantly defend, almost forking her.

After her night of possessed puking? Even Linda Blair couldn't have done better. I'm surprised Claire can even eat right now. I should have warned her not to swallow the wine. I'm just glad she's feeling better after close to twelve hours of sleep and a bowl of chicken soup at midnight.

"Hey!" she says, yanking her hand away. "I just wanted a taste."

"You're telling me you're still hungry after all that?" I ask, eyes traveling over the empty plates covering every inch of space on our table.

"What can I say? They have small serving sizes here."

She's wearing the jacket I gave her. It sits so well on her shoulders that I'm glad I bought it for her. She is pulling off effortlessly chic.

When she lent it to me yesterday, it absolutely smelled of her. And was warm like her. I didn't want to take it off, but it would have been weird if I didn't return it. So return it I did.

Moods lighter from the hearty combination of carbs and excessive amounts of cheese, Pullen gathers the group of us for a walking tour around the town to burn off some of the calories. It's a short stroll from the gates of the chateau. In fact, Chateau Blanc might be the biggest property around, and the town surrounds it.

The pleasant and calming scent of baking bread wafts straight from the bakeries into the air. It mixes with the delicious aroma of roasted chicken slathered in the most decadent butter. Both intermingle with the lingering acrid, musty fog of cigarette smoke. And underneath it all is the freshness of wet grass. I breathe in deeply, unlocking precious memories of night walks with my parents.

Today is in many ways similar to those nights, but the major difference is I walk along cobblestone streets with someone who intrigues me. I see this as a chance to get to know her better.

I move my gaze toward Claire, who ambles along with her hands in the pockets of her jacket, and say, "When I dreamed of traveling, I never thought I'd find myself in such a lovely place."

"It's like walking in a painting, that's for sure," Claire says while looking round.

When the group reaches a bridge, Pullen asks, "Does anyone know about the legend of the love locks?"

Parker raises his hand. "It's where couples etch their initials on the face of the locks. Then they attach the lock to the railing of a bridge for the entire world to see. Afterward, they throw the key into the river."

Pullen nods. "*Bon.* Well done, Monsieur Parker."

"Why do they throw away the key?" Claire asks.

"It is the ultimate symbol of forever because the lock can never be opened ever again."

I have read story after story on the internet about couples who traveled from all over the world just to come to Paris and attach a lock. Some of them even used their life savings for a once-in-a-lifetime opportunity to show their love for each other. The couples with us practically swoon on the spot, so caught up are they in Pullen's words.

"Isn't that tradition only in Paris?" I ask.

"Sadly, the government has banned the tradition of love locks because the railings on the bridges started collapsing due to the weight of the locks," Pullen explains. "But here, in the town of Montsoreau, we have created our own tradition. We have small bottles of wine from this year's vintage. You and your significant other will write your names on the labels of the bottles. We have already taken the liberty of etching your initials onto the cork. Then we will place the bottles in a private cellar beneath the bridge. Right under the Loire River."

A weight falls to the pit of my stomach. I'm starting to see where this is about to go without Pullen having to say another word. I start thinking of all the ways I can back out of this and find none that won't make things way too obvious.

"We at Chateau Blanc have provided everything you might need to share your love for one another." Pullen gestures toward her assistant, who stands by a table at the foot of the bridge. There is a stairway beyond that goes down to where I assume the cellar is. "Please take your bottle, write your names, then we will cork it and store it. During a milestone in your relationship, you are welcome to return, retrieve your bottle, and enjoy your very own vintage." She points at the stone bridge a few yards away. "And do not worry—this cellar is owned by the chateau and will not be disturbed, so your love will also stand the test of time."

One by one, each couple with us takes their bottle and cork and moves toward the bridge. Without consulting me, Claire moves forward and takes a bottle and a Sharpie and the cork with our initials on it. She shows them to me.

"What do you say?" she asks. "Do you want to write our names and I'll cork the bottle? I'm stronger than I look."

"What are you doing?" I hiss, looking around to see if anyone of our group is close by.

Claire blinks at me, confused. "If you want to cork the bottle, I'll write our names, no problem. Although I have to warn you, my handwriting is equivalent to chicken scratch."

"That's not what I mean." I sigh. "We're not really together."

For a second, an emotion I don't understand flits over Claire's face before she covers it up with a smile. "Then I don't see the problem."

"What do you mean?"

"We're not together, so it shouldn't matter if we put the wine in the cellar. It doesn't mean a thing."

"You're not making any sense."

"Look." Claire breathes out. "It's simple. If we don't participate, then Parker will get suspicious and he will tell Bob. They'll think that something is wrong, because why wouldn't a happy couple want a symbol of their love fermenting in an underground cellar? Are you prepared to answer all of those questions?"

She's got me there. "Well, no."

"Then isn't it just easier to go with everything they have planned for us this week instead of hesitating every step of the way?"

A shrug lifts out of me. "I guess."

"Anyway, this doesn't mean anything, right? It's a made-up tradition from a chateau that hopes to be a tourist destination."

I open my mouth to say something, but the words fail me. When I read about love locks, I found the tradition absolutely romantic. It actually originated in Serbia and eventually made its way to Paris. I honestly thought that if I ever joined a tradition like that it would be because I have someone I love standing by my side.

But I also see the logic in Claire's words. We're supposed to be the picture of a happy couple. It's just a week. How hard can that be? Then, after Bob offers the partnership to me, Claire and I will suddenly break up and call off the engagement and go our separate ways. Easy peasy.

"Fine," I say, pushing down the urge to resist. "You cork and I'll write our names. I have better penmanship."

"See? How hard was that?" Claire winks at me before she turns around and makes her way to the bridge.

My feet feel rooted to the ground. The weight in my stomach gets heavier, preventing me from moving.

"Dina!" Parker calls, waving me over.

No, I find myself thinking, it's not easy at all. In fact, adding the wine to the collection in the cellar is probably one of the hardest things I have to do.

Because maybe, just maybe, I want the tradition to work its magic. I believe in wanting my love to get better as it ages—like fine wine. I want to come back here one day, many years down the road, uncork that bottle, and taste the sweetness of my feelings for that person.

The question is… is Claire that forever?

Her retreating back feels so far away.

Then, just as suddenly, she's back at my side, taking my hand, and with a bright smile on her face, she pulls me forward. I take a step. Then another, and another, and in no time she has me giggling, forgetting for the moment the confusion choking me up inside.

CHAPTER EIGHTEEN

Claire

FOR THE rest of the afternoon, our group ambles from stall to stall in the open market at the town's center. I marvel at the veritable treasure trove of locally produced specialties and imported delicacies.

The ingredients being sold are so fresh I can almost taste the smoked ham, the greenest vegetables, and the most pungent cheeses just by looking at them. But none of that matters. It still niggles at me how resistant Dina was to adding our bottle of wine into the cellar of love. I mean, sure we're faking it, but she didn't have to act like writing our names on a wine bottle was the last thing she wanted to do with me.

Insert laugh track here. I thought we shared a moment at the wine tasting yesterday when I lent her my jacket. And at the chateau bar the other night? We really got to know each other. Had some laughs. We connected.

I hate myself for dwelling. Sure, it's just a stupid tradition. It's not the end of the world. I should be on cloud nine—Dina sent me all the details for the comedy festival, and I then forwarded them to Dwight. I'm all set to perform in Edinburgh. But no.

My eyes find Dina moving to a stall selling freshly made pasta.

"Hi," she says, smiling at the pretty girl behind the counter.

"Hi, I'm Margot. What can I do for you?" she asks in lilting French-accented English that sounds… nice.

"I like your accent."

She blushes and giggles. "I bet you say that to all the girls."

The way she says *girl* sounds as if it has an *e* instead.

Dina clears her throat and says, "I just meant the French speak beautifully."

"Then you should hear us sing."

A scowl forms on my face as I move to stand beside Dina. "She's pretty."

"Margot actually—"

"Margot?" I say the name like a curse word, remembering Charmaine from the Greasy Spoon slipping Dina her number. I don't think Dina realizes it, but she's like catnip to women.

"That's me," the girl says.

"Will you excuse us?" I ask her and she nods.

I take Dina by the arm and move away from the stall. Dina looks over her shoulder and waves at her, smiling. Margot waves back.

"Will you stop it!" I snap.

Dina returns her attention to me. "What's with the tone?"

"Don't pretend like you don't know what you're doing."

"Usually being around food puts you in a good mood. Something happen?"

Oh, something did happen. "What's with the flirting back there?"

A tick begins along Dina's jaw. "Who said anything about flirting? I was just admiring the pasta and her accent."

"Just admit that you were flirting and be done with it. Like that time with Charmaine."

"Charmaine?" She has the gall to look confused.

"At the diner in New York!"

"Claire." Dina pinches the bridge of her nose and sighs. "I wasn't flirting. I was about to ask Margot if she knew of a place where we can have dinner."

"What?" All urges to pick a fight dissipate.

"It doesn't matter now since I just spotted a pub behind you."

"Pub?" My eyebrow arches.

"I want to eat somewhere else for tonight. Is that so bad?"

Not wanting to show how embarrassed I feel, I say, "Well, lead the way to this pub."

Dina goes around me and points. The brick-and-mortar facade of the pub blends in with the other buildings on either side of it. In all caps, a wooden sign spells out *Lucky's* in green. I trail Dina inside as a gust of wind forces us to rush. The temperature drops with the sun.

We look around the simple entryway. There's a stained-glass window on one side that looks out to nowhere. Beside it is a frame with a man in uniform saluting and the words *If you are an Irishman, your place is with your chums under the flags.* Indeed, the saluting man stands beneath an assortment of flags in the picture. And below the frame is a sign that reads *Guinness since 1945*. On the other wall is a tile mosaic that features different bottles of beer.

"Well, hello!" A woman with flaming red hair sashays toward us, wearing a half apron over faded jeans. Her black T-shirt stretches over massive breasts. To say she's curvy underestimates the full package. "Welcome to Lucky's. I'm Gwen."

"Hello," Dina says. "We're staying over at Chateau—"

"Tired of the fancy food, huh?" Her smile is just as wide as Margot's.

"Yes," I say. "We'd like a table for two, please."

Her gaze moves between us. "Americans?"

Dina nods. "We're here for the rest of the week."

"Well, then." She smooths her hands over her apron. "It's not every day we get such a beautiful couple in here."

"Oh, we're not—" I begin to say.

Dina puts an arm around my shoulders. "See, honey. I told you we weren't lost. She's been in a mood all day," she finishes, addressing Gwen.

"Well, we can sure fix that here." Gwen pats Dina on the shoulder. "You've come to the place with the best Irish food in France."

"Irish food?" I blurt out.

"Why yes," Gwen says. "My family came for a vacation and simply never left. We've been making Guinness pie since—"

"1945," Dina supplies.

"Exactly! You two make a darling couple. I knew the instant you walked in. Well, come, come, I have a table waiting for you."

She sashays away.

"What the hell are you doing?" I whisper-hiss.

"Smell that?" Dina sniffs the air. Scents of barley mixed with sautéing garlic and onions and all the good things a person can eat and drink. "I love this place already."

She ushers me after Gwen into the cozy dark-wood interior. A massive bar takes up half the floor area. The space isn't big at all, giving the place a hearty atmosphere. The wood gleams around us, set off by soft lighting coming from an iron chandelier. We stop at a table nestled in a warm corner surrounded by more magnificent stained-glass windows.

I reluctantly take a seat. What is Dina playing at here?

"Now, will you let me order for you?" Gwen asks. "I have a special meal I have planned for lovebirds."

I barely stifle a flinch at the word *lovebirds* as Dina nods, thanking Gwen. It's ironic that the glass windows depict couples in amorous embraces while I inwardly freak out about Dina pretending to be my girlfriend/fake fiancée. Where did that come from? It's like the universe is mocking me.

When the words "green beer" leave Gwen's lips, my attention returns to the conversation. "I didn't think they served green beer outside of St. Patrick's Day."

"Oh, we serve it all the time here," Gwen says. "It's part of what makes the place touristy."

"As much as I want to...." I pause, my stomach protesting the memories of my wine intoxication from yesterday. "I'm not drinking tonight, thank you."

"We can make it out of ginger ale if you prefer."

I nod as she finishes jotting down the order, then saunters away. Dina shrugs out of her jacket and leans back, taking in the place.

Not knowing what to do with the silence between us that isn't exactly awkward but isn't entirely comfortable either, I ask, "What did Gwen order for us?"

A delectable smirk gives Dina's features a mischievous edge. "Steak and Guinness pie. Then Irish coffee and Guinness cake for dessert."

At the mention of Guinness, I groan. "You're trying to get me drunk again, aren't you? Just admit it."

"The Irish coffee is for me. Gwen will give you just the regular brew. The alcohol in the Guinness is burned away in the cooking process. You won't get buzzed." Dina reaches across the table and brings my knuckles to her lips.

I pull my hand away as if burned despite the ripple of pleasure running all over my body. "Stop it."

"What?" she asks.

"Making an ass of yourself."

"That's not—"

"Hear yah go," Gwen says, interrupting the rest of what Dina is saying as she sets down two heaping plates of steak and Guinness pie and what looks like gallon-size pints of the green beer. "Enjoy."

I wait for Dina to finish what she was about to say, but her attention is fully captured by all the food.

She brings a spoonful of beef into her mouth and closes her eyes. "Mmm. This is so good."

Amazed by her reaction, I bring my own spoon to my mouth. I all but forget our previous conversation. The meat is so tender it practically melts on my tongue. The stew is thick with the taste of onions and rosemary and thyme. My eyes practically roll to the back of my head the moment I taste the robustness of the Guinness.

Dina's right. The alcohol is gone, but the creamy, spicy flavor of the brew remains. It's like coffee and chocolate mixed together with Worcestershire sauce. Sounds disgusting, but it's actually good.

"I wasn't making an ass of myself." Dina takes a long draught of her beer.

"I'm sorry?" I tilt my head.

"Earlier you said I was making an ass of myself."

Ah, what was left unsaid before the food came. "And what do you call all that?"

"An attempt to make you smile."

The green ginger ale goes down the wrong pipe, causing me to lapse into a coughing fit that prevents an answer. Good thing too, because I have no idea how I should respond.

"From the looks of your plates, it's safe to say you like the food," Gwen says as she swaps our empty dishes for a single slice of Guinness cake and our cups of coffee with whipped cream on top. "Are you all right, m'dear?"

I cough one more time, then squeak out, "Fine. Just fine."

"Well, dessert is on the house."

"Gwen, you're so sweet." Dina picks up a fork and takes a pinch of the cake.

She giggles. "You two just look so adorable. I can't help myself."

I shift in my seat, unable to meet anyone's gaze until a fork with a morsel of cake hovers just below my lips. I glance at Dina, who's smiling from ear to ear.

"Here you go, honeybuns. The first bite is for you."

"Excuse me," I say, slapping my hands on the table and standing up fast.

"Something wrong?" Gwen asks, concern all over her round face.

"I need to use the restroom," I stammer out, not looking at Dina.

"Over by the back."

She hasn't even finished gesturing when I run toward the sign illuminated with stick figures. It's a unisex bathroom, I realize when I push in and lock the door. Not really needing to relieve myself, I stumble to the sink. I push up the tap and cup my hands under the running water. Then I splash my overheated face.

Breathing hard, droplets streaming down my cheeks, I stare into the mirror. I can't get the words *an attempt to make you smile* out of my head. Clearly all of Dina's pretending comes from a good place. Right? So I shouldn't be pissed. But for a moment there—just a tiny moment—I wanted it all to be real.

I'M IN bed totally bewildered while Dina sleeps soundly beside me. I should be asleep, but I'm wide-awake. I have my leg akimbo and I'm twirling a lock of my hair.

The dinner at the pub should have been a one-off. I put on a smile when I returned to the table so Dina wouldn't be embarrassed. I didn't want her to feel betrayed by me.

Feelings of wanting to back out of this fake relationship plague me again. The longer this agreement between us lasts, the more pretending to be together wouldn't be good for either of us. Or maybe I'm the only one who will fall apart after this if I don't guard my heart, but the universe has other plans, it seems.

After today, I don't think her boss will believe that we broke up and canceled the engagement during this trip. Because of my need to please and my natural personality, my inclination to perform, I've managed to dig myself into an even bigger, deeper hole. There's definitely no backing out now.

I'm staring at the ceiling trying to figure out my next steps. I haven't had a vacation since I started getting serious with my stand-up. I travel, sure, but that's always for work. Putting your name out there means going from state to state and playing at all the different comedy clubs.

Based on what Dwight tells me during our calls, I'm doing well. I'm bringing in more people and my shows are selling out. That's always good news for a comic who wants to make it in this business.

Performing at Edinburgh will definitely open doors for me. And that opportunity came from Dina. With all the women I've dated, I thought pretending to be Dina's fiancée would be easy.

But there's something about Dina that pulls me in every time I get near her. She's like the sun, and I guess I'm a chunk of space rock. I was content to travel the universe until I got within her orbit. Her gravitational pull has reeled me in and refuses to let go. I've never met anyone quite like her.

Eventually my eyes grow heavy. My breathing becomes steadier. Until I finally close my eyes and drift off to sleep. My last thought of the night is the pleasure of seeing the blush on Dina's face when I took her hand and pulled her toward the bridge where everyone waited.

THE NEXT day I wake up to a call from the front desk and a note from Dina saying she went to the gym and that we'll meet for breakfast at the lounge. With my lifestyle, I'm never one to wake up early. In fact, on most days, I get up right about noon. As much as my body begs for more sleep, my stomach doesn't want to miss out on breakfast.

I get dressed and stuff the clothes I wore yesterday into the hamper. Dina convinced me to try having my clothes professionally laundered. I reluctantly agreed despite freaking out about handing over my used underwear to a complete stranger. It was either that or hanging my washed underwear in the bathroom to dry. Dina might not approve.

I realize my thoughts keep coming back to her. I wonder what she's doing. Is she still at the gym? Is she thinking about me too?

Since this day will be packed with more activities, I wear the jacket that Dina gave me again. This time, I pick out a light sweater and slacks combination that came with the clothes from the Mustard Seed.

When I'm dressed, my phone rings. Dwight's name flashes on the screen. I take a seat on the couch beside the indoor plant with leaves that look like plastic right as my phone pings in between rings. It's a picture from Dina. It's of the both of us sharing the chocolate cake from our first night at the chateau.

A smile stretches my lips. It's a sweet picture. The next message says that our picture is blowing up on the social media posts of the travel agency. Apparently everyone loves the picture. Good.

I finally pick up my phone and say, "Hey, Dwight. How's it hanging?"

"Claire," he says in that smooth-as-silk voice of his. "I finally have the press release out for your slot at Edinburgh. It's gaining a lot of traction. Being a last-minute inclusion is actually working for you."

"That's great," I say, downplaying the excitement going through me. "I'm already reviewing my set and seeing what to include for my act."

"That's a good call. Being a part of the Edinburgh Comedy Festival can only do good things for your career."

I bite the inside of my cheek. "I'm actually really looking forward to it."

"Because of this news, theaters are asking to book you," Dwight says. "Which puts us in a good position to pitch your special to Netflix."

Hearing that makes my stomach flip. "This day just keeps getting better."

"Which is why taking your Fat, Fun, and Single show on the road is the best strategy for us right now. A proper tour."

"What if I'm not single anymore?" I ask, because it's an important question considering my current circumstances.

There's a long pause before Dwight bursts into peals of laughter.

"It's not that funny," I say.

He breathes hard in order to regain his composure, but even then, small giggles still bubble out of him. I wait, forcing myself not to roll my eyes. Is it really that comical to think that I might eventually find someone to be in a relationship with?

Dwight finally settles down and says, "That's flat-out not going to work. Your entire act is based on you being single. It's what you're most popular for."

Then I guess he shouldn't see the picture of me and Dina sharing chocolate cake. He might have a stroke. But I think I'm safe there, since my world and Dina's are far enough apart that they won't collide. Plus, I'm not famous enough for the tabloids to pick up my story. We'll see after Edinburgh.

"What do you think about going on tour? We'll need your decision soon because we'll have to put the logistics together," Dwight says, returning to the main topic of our conversation. "We'll need to book the theaters and put the tickets out on sale."

"Sounds good to me, but let me think about it first," I say, then push up off the couch.

"Don't think too long on it, Claire," Dwight says, and I end the call.

The potential tour is exactly what's on my mind as I make my way to breakfast, running through my set for Edinburgh. What would being with Dina mean for my career? Fake engagement or not, I really think I'm starting to have feelings for her.

We definitely have nothing in common, but somehow we fit together perfectly. I can already feel my heart breaking, because a relationship with someone like her is exactly what I've always wanted. Now it seems more and more like I can never have what I want.

CHAPTER NINETEEN

Dina

CHATEAU BLANC stands tall and proud at the center of a large number of knot gardens, square gardens bordered by box hedging, and these are filled in with different plants to create a beautiful, very symmetrical layout. The whole area covers nine hectares and includes a water garden with ponds and fountains, an ornamental garden with intricate patterns of clipped boxes filled with different flowers according to the seasons, and an enormous vegetable garden.

It seems that at every corner, flowers bloom out of the earth in an explosion of color. From the massive trees to the babbling brook running through the property, the grounds are manicured and well-appointed. Dappled sunlight glints off the greenest leaves I've ever seen.

Unfortunately, the splendor of the place is having a hard time competing with the turbulence in my mind. What the hell was I thinking? After the pub last night, one would think that I would learn my lesson: keep my growing feelings to myself.

Claire isn't interested, if her reaction last night can be trusted. She ran out of the dining room so fast it gave me whiplash. But I'm pretty sure we shared a spark of something.

It's driving me crazy. Claire might have meant the love wine as a joke. A way to get me to relax about being in one of the most romantic places on this earth. I know this. Yet I still find myself walking by her side today. Ready to go on the next adventure Pullen has in store for us. Something about ringing a bell at a tower.

"Only those brave enough to climb to the very top of the tower will be granted it," Pullen says, walking backward so she can address the group as we move.

"Granted what?" I ask absentmindedly.

I'm too preoccupied with glancing sideways at Claire. Despite what happened last night, she looks more relaxed than I am.

"Everlasting love," Pullen clarifies as we stroll along a path toward the tower attached to a chapel. "You will have to ring the bell three times, holding the rope together."

I cluck my tongue. "That's nothing."

"You sure?" Claire says, eyeing me.

I ignore her skepticism as we enter the chapel. I'm here to enjoy myself. I finally accepted that last night. I will take whatever comes of it.

Galvanized by the purity of my feelings, I face the climb that will eventually lead us to the top of the tower with determination.

"I have to admit, this is cool," Claire says.

The pure joy on her face touches me deeply. I remind myself to stay present in the moment as we navigate a spiral staircase that takes us to yet another level. The last thing I want is to miss actually experiencing the place with Claire. Goose bumps rise on my arms as we walk the corridors of old. Some of the walls are rough, while others are as smooth as polished marble.

We visit many rooms and pause to enjoy the view at each window. The higher we go, the more we can see of the countryside. I begin to imagine the chateau as it was in its heyday, my mind conjuring up a multitude of maids, warriors, kings, and queens strolling along its halls.

"I've never seen anything like it," I say in awe as we come to the main room of the chapel with its vaulted ceilings and ornate altar.

Claire looks up and turns in a circle. Then she touches my shoulder, forcing me to look her in the eyes.

"Come on." Claire looks over her shoulder and grins, gesturing toward another door by tilting her head. "We're here."

So caught up in experiencing the tower, I totally forgot the purpose of our climb. I let Claire lead the way. My brain can only focus on moving one foot in front of the other.

Bright sunlight replaces the dimness of the tower's interior. I squint against the glare, shielding my eyes by placing my hand over them. A wonderful breeze ruffles my hair. This day couldn't be any more perfect if doves flew in a V above us.

Since we're the last to arrive at the top, the rest of our group has already formed a line to ring the bell. Claire keeps her body directly in front of me as we inch forward. Once my eyes adjust to the sunlight, my gaze falls to the back of Claire's neck. In a momentary lapse of sanity,

I find myself wondering what it would feel like to weave my fingers through her hair.

Tempted by the idea of touching Claire, I don't notice that we've reached the front of the line until someone says my name. I blink back into reality only to find everyone staring expectantly at me—Claire. Bob and Parker, and the man in a windbreaker standing by the rope attached to a large bell hanging above us. Its copper has long since turned green with age.

"All right," Claire says with a shrug. "Let's do this."

"Wait—" I reach out.

Claire holds on to the rope with both hands. My heart pounds against my rib cage. I can't find my breath. My chest constricts painfully. A part of me wants to pull Claire's hands away from the rope. The other part of me is rooted in place, unable to move a single muscle.

The breeze is no longer soothing. It turns into a gust that dries the cold sweat dotting my brow. I attempt to swallow, but the walls of my throat refuse to move. A small keening sound reaches my ears.

"Claire," I whisper.

CHAPTER TWENTY

Claire

A RUSH of adrenaline courses through my body as I wait for Dina to hold the rope with me. A sense of danger and accomplishment whirls inside me—like gaining a superpower. It makes me feel like I can do anything. We stand several stories up with nothing but thin rails between us and a multistory fall in a tower that stood the test of time but could also crumble beneath our feet at any minute.

Then again, someone would have to be terribly unlucky to actually fall. Or for the stone to just collapse. It's safe or we wouldn't be allowed up here, but I can't deny the thrill that still goes through me while we stand at the top of the tower that looks out to the chateau's gardens and beyond.

I let out a whoop and bounce on the balls of my feet. "Come on, Dina. What are you waiting for?"

The other partners cheer, egging us on. Even the assistant joins in with encouraging words. Then my gaze lands on a pale Dina. All my excitement vanishes faster than a magician in a cloud of smoke.

"Dina?" I rush to her side. "What's wrong?"

Dina shakes her head. Her eyes focus on a far-off point, her pupils tiny pinpricks. I remember her telling me that when she was a kid, Dina climbed a tree to escape being found during a hide-and-seek game. She doesn't come across as someone afraid of heights. She seemed fine climbing up here. What could have caused her to shut down and panic?

"Dina," I say as calmly as my racing heart will allow. "Dina, look at me."

In the slowest five seconds ever, Dina's eyes move to focus on mine before she whispers, "Claire...."

Her voice is such a small sound, but it's something.

"Happens all the time," the assistant says.

Ignoring the concern quickly spreading around us, I place my hands on either side of Dina's face and guide her head so our eyes can lock.

"Breathe, Dina." I take an exaggerated breath. "See? Concentrate on my breathing. That's it."

Soon shaking fingers reach out and clutch the front of my shirt. I wait, unmoving.

It takes another couple of seconds before Dina's breathing evens out enough for her to say, "I don't know what came over me."

"No ringing the bell for you." I roll my eyes. "Come on." I nod at the others to indicate I've got this, and they go on ahead of us.

"I feel like such a failure," Dina says once we are back inside.

I take the lead, as the narrow staircase only allows for one person at a time to descend. "You're not a failure. No one will care about ringing some stupid bell. It's fine."

Dina huffs a sad laugh. "How hard is it to hold on to a rope? I don't understand. One minute I'm fine and then the next I can't move."

"Hey, let it go. This is not a competition."

"Isn't that what Pullen said earlier? That only the brave will be granted everlasting love?" She sniffs. "I feel like such a failure. What if Bob suspects?"

"Hey." I turn around to face her, looking up at her beautiful face, wrinkled in concern. "You're not a failure. You don't lose anything by not ringing the bell."

"You don't understand," she says, biting her lip as if to keep herself from saying more.

"Spit it out."

"It's just...." Dina drops her gaze and sighs. "It's just when I saw you reaching for the rope, I was sure you would fall. But I was so scared that I couldn't move. What happens if you're ever dangling from a cliff and I'm the only one there to save you and I freeze up and I can't save you and you fall?"

"Uh, okay. Are you hearing yourself?"

Shaking her head harder this time, Dina says, "But what if—"

"Dina, focus," I cut her off. "Nowhere in our lives will we ever be in the position of dangling off a cliff. I will not allow it."

Like she did at the parapet, Dina blinks. The clarity in her eyes says she is beginning to understand how irrational she's being.

"Now, take a deep breath. That's it. And let it out slowly." When Dina does what I ask, a corner of my lips lifts. "Next time no more death-defying acts, agreed?"

"Promise." She nods once, looking steadier on her feet. "No more."

"Good." Turning back around, I continue our descent. "Let's get out of here. Risking my life made me hungry."

"So not funny."

CHAPTER TWENTY-ONE

Dina

THE PICNIC the next day involves games. Couple-centric games. Against the pretty backdrop of Chateau Blanc's flower garden with its tall pines, topiaries, and statues. The day couldn't be more geared toward romance if it was Valentine's Day and not the middle of the year.

Standing side by side with Claire, I look up at the perfect concentration on her face—brows drawn tight and all.

"You sure about this?" I ask with equal seriousness.

She nods once, then hooks her arm around my waist to grip my hip. The strength of her hold gives me the confidence I need to grab the back of her shirt. Someone yells, "Go!"

In one heave, I lift Claire against my side and we take off at a gallop in the three-legged race she convinced me to join.

Squealing in delight, she lets me do most of the work since I'm taller, content to hang on for dear life. The spectators cheer, including Pullen, who jumps in place. She cheers for everyone participating.

Our only real competition is Bob and Parker. The excitement in the air spurs me to kick faster with the leg currently tied against Claire's.

Laughter booms out of me when we reach the finish line at the same time as my boss and his husband. We all trip over one another, but before I can fall, Claire wraps me in her arms and twists so I land on top of her. Curses and giggles abound.

As I lean up, my eyes immediately lock with hers, and suddenly it's like standing in the eye of a storm. A pause happens between us amid all the excitement and congratulatory shouts. Beneath my hand, I can feel the rapid beats of her heart. She sucks in a breath and, in a quick move, heaves us both to our feet and begins untying our legs.

"Do you think we won?" I ask.

"Yes, we did," Claire announces.

"I object!" Bob and Parker say in unison, already untied.

I still get a kick out of seeing the two of them together. If there is a perfect couple in this entire group, it's Parker and Bob. All it takes is to see how they look at each other or how they hover around each other, one never too far away. Secretly, I wish I could have that.

"We clearly won by a toe!" Parker points out.

"Dina crossed the finish line before you," Claire rebuts. "So if there's anyone winning by a toe, it would be us."

"Yeah, you." Bob pokes her shoulder good-naturedly. "Don't think I didn't see Dina doing all the work, hauling you like a sack of potatoes."

"Hey!" I join in, unable to help myself. Everyone is having so much fun.

Bob grins at me. "A pretty sack of potatoes."

I lift my chin and grin. "As long as we understand each other."

"That's still cheating," Parker challenges loud enough for everyone gathered to hear.

According to the mix of jubilation and objection, the crowd is clearly divided. The energy in the air sends tingles of excitement over my skin. I have never enjoyed myself this much.

"Pullen!" Parker calls. "You be the tiebreaker here."

"Boo!" Claire says through cupped hands. "You know Pullen is biased. She clearly likes you better."

"Let's call it even," Bob suggests, having been reduced to chuckles.

"Never!" both Claire and Parker shout at the same time.

Pullen suggests a pie-eating contest. This goes over well with the mob. In under a minute, Claire and Parker sit beside each other on a picnic bench with a pie tin each in front of them on the table. Bob walks among those gathered to watch, taking bets of all things. Of course I put myself down for ten on Claire.

"All right," Pullen says. She stands at the other side of the table in front of the competitors, who bump shoulders with each other. "The rules are simple. No use of hands. The first one to finish eating the pie wins." Then she gives the floor to me.

Biting my lip, I glance at Claire, who gives me a wink and grin. The combination wakes flutters in my belly.

"Ready," I say. Claire and Parker share a look. "Set." I raise my hand and drop it at "Go!"

Claire and Parker plunge their faces into the pies—cherry for Claire, freshly picked from the gardens this morning, and apple for

Parker brought in from Paris, according to the chef. The crowd cheers for their respective bets.

I dance on my toes, egging Claire on to chew faster. I clap when half her pie is gone in what seems like seconds. She moves her face around the tin until nothing is left, then pushes off the table and raises both her arms above her head and roars. The lower half of her face is red.

Everyone screams with her, including myself. I catch the naughty spark in her eyes too late, because she's already on me, smearing cherry filling all over my face. I shriek and laugh at the same time.

Claire's arms around my waist keep me from getting away. In my struggle, Claire trips, sending the both of us to the grass. The breath in my lungs comes out in an *oof* and giggles.

I take out a handkerchief from my pocket and start wiping her mouth. She stills, allowing my ministrations. We look into each other's eyes.

Thirty minutes later, with faces washed, Claire and I enter another game. We come away from the egg toss second. Bob and Parker joined this one too and win uncontested.

By the third game, which involves a version of blind man's bluff where someone is blindfolded and must find their partner from a group by listening for their voice calling their partner's name, I get a sense of just how competitive Parker and Bob are.

Claire bets Parker a thousand dollars she can find me in less than a minute. Parker takes the bet and doubles it. My head spins.

I pull Claire aside and say, "Are you sure about this? That's a lot of money."

Her eyebrow lifts. "Only if I don't win."

"How sure are you that you'll win?"

She winks at me. "We got this."

At first I want no part in this silly competition of theirs, but when Claire said she would use the money to buy her travel tickets to Edinburgh and book a hotel stay, I quickly agreed. Depending on the mode of travel she uses and the kind of hotel she books, that money can certainly be well spent. Not to mention any incidentals along the way that she might need.

I want her to be comfortable during her trip. Two grand can buy her the best seats on any train, bus, and taxi she chooses; especially if I book it for her. She'll have so much left over she can even do some shopping.

So, standing with nine other women in a circle, Claire at the center, I clear my throat. I need to be loud enough for Claire to hear me.

Pullen stands behind Claire and places a silk scarf over her eyes, tying the ends at the back of her head. Then she tests Claire by making faces. Claire merely rolls her shoulders and neck like a fighter waiting for the bell, oblivious to Pullen's antics. Parker, meanwhile, cues up the stopwatch on his cell phone and shouts one minute, as if Claire needs a reminder. The taunt earns him the finger.

I bite the inside of my cheek to keep the laughter in. We have to stay quiet until the game officially starts. To add more of a challenge, Pullen spins Claire in place three times. At Claire's third rotation, Pullen lets her go and the game is on.

All ten of us call out Claire's name. None of us can approach her. I rock on the balls of my feet, saying her name over and over again.

For what seems like an eternity, Claire doesn't move from where she stands. She tilts her head one way then the other. The flutters in my stomach intensify, radiating from inside my belly to manifest as goose bumps on my skin.

Even as I say her name, I mentally will her toward me. Not because of the bet. Not for the two grand. I genuinely want her to find me, see if she can pick out my voice from nine other women.

"Claire!" Her name sounds shrill to my ears at this point.

The excitement in the air is getting to me. Like a drug, I draw from it, charging my senses to the point of overload. The sunset seems brighter. The leaves seem greener, the sky bluer. The air sweeter. I take all of it in as electric shocks running beneath my skin.

At the forty-five-second mark, Claire still hasn't moved. I'm at the end of my patience. My excitement reaches a painful peak in my chest. When I call her name again, she tilts her head toward me.

That's when everything changes.

As sure as the sun rises in the east, Claire turns toward me and walks with confidence until she reaches me. Without removing the blindfold, she lifts me into the air. My squeal of surprise turns into giggles. She found me.

Whistles and catcalls rain on us.

"You better be Dina or I'm genuinely screwed," Claire says, planting a kiss on my cheek.

"Good thing." I yank off the scarf so I can drown in her eyes. "How did you do that?"

"I have my talents." She grins, blinking repeatedly as if to clear her vision.

"You totally cheated!" Parker accuses when he reaches our side.

Claire shakes her head, never taking her gaze from my face. "I told you. I can find her in under a minute. What was the time?"

"Just under a minute," Parker grumbles.

"Be ready to pay up." Her eyes burn bright. "I'm buying something special for my girl besides those tickets to Edinburgh."

Her girl.

Those words haunt me for the rest of the afternoon until the sky darkens enough for the fireworks. The party winding down does nothing to alleviate the jitters of energy crawling beneath my skin. Nothing seems to calm my racing heart.

I know I need to come down, but I don't want to. The conviction in Claire's words worries me. I suspect she wasn't playacting when she said them.

When Claire insists we walk along the brook, I don't resist. How can I when she looks at me like I'm the only woman at the party?

The way her eyes seem to shine almost like liquid twists my insides. I let her take my hand.

We leave our shoes on the grass. The water reaching my ankles cools my too-hot skin. Today has been too much. More than all the other events combined.

The first spear shoots up into the sky. Upon reaching its peak, it explodes into spider legs of light. Claire stops and looks up. I do the same.

The next spear quickly follows and spreads like a dandelion. The third one pops and sparkles. A kind of choreography emerges.

A symphony of blues and greens and reds interspersed with dazzling gold. Soon the entire night sky lights up with blossom upon blossom of pyrotechnic light. The show draws enthusiastic "oohs" and "aahs" along with claps and laughter.

The more time we spend together, the more I see a change in Claire. Maybe I see a change in me too. We're less guarded somehow. I can't explain the feeling exactly. Comfortable. Relaxed.

Then, at the height of the show, Claire faces me. Cupping my cheek, she runs the pad of her thumb over my lower lip. My breath hitches.

"If I kiss you right now, will it save you?" Claire asks.

I know I shouldn't. That giving in would be reckless… for the both of us. But I tilt my head down in response to her touch.

This is the biggest mistake we can make in our fake relationship. I see it in Claire's eyes too, yet neither of us speaks before she lifts up and takes what I offer.

She kisses the way she smiles when she looks at me, slow and easy. Gentle yet demanding a response. And respond I do, tasting the tartness of the lemon iced tea she favored all afternoon. She cradles the back of my neck, tracing the line of my jaw with her thumb as if she wants to remember its shape.

When she takes my bottom lip between her teeth, I wrap my arms around her shoulders to keep from falling. For a first kiss, amid the fireworks exploding above us, it is amazing. Each pass our lips make tugs at me, begging me to draw her closer. It's as if an invisible string binds her heart to mine, and no matter what happens, nothing can cut the connection between us.

For the briefest instant, as she whispers my name against my mouth and I whisper hers back, I catch a glimpse of the future. Just a glimmer, not clear enough to see properly. Like a mirage in the desert. It frightens me enough to remind me that our time together is finite. So, after a final brush of my lips against hers, I step out of the circle of her arms and look up at the riot of color bursting in the night sky.

Chapter Twenty-Two

Claire

I WAKE up to a knocking. I squint my eyes open only to realize the knocking is in my head. All that wine I consumed is finally catching up with me. The French like their wine. At every meal we eat, there's at least a bottle or two consumed. Even though I made it a point to pace myself at dinner last night, my head feels three sizes too big for my neck and weighs a ton.

I roll over to my side. The crunch of leather tells me I might have slept on my jacket. As I push up, I press a hand against my forehead to ensure that my head remains attached to my body.

The robe I'm wearing has shifted, leaving me partially naked. The towel that was on my head now lies abandoned on the pillow. Dry yet matted strands of my hair try to tumble over my shoulders, but they remain springy. I think I'm going to need to take another shower just to be able to comb it out.

First I need to stop the marching band playing like it's the Macy's Thanksgiving Day Parade in my head. I push up from a seated position to my feet. I wobble a moment. I lock my knees and wait.

The honeymoon suite's room spins a couple of times. I close my eyes, reach for the trash can, and brace myself for the coming puke. Seconds later, nothing climbs up my throat. I take that as a good sign.

Opening my eyes again, this time slowly, I make my way to the bathroom. I wash my face. I pick up a towel from a stack and dry myself. I look at my reflection in the mirror and grimace.

I look like fresh roadkill. And I certainly feel like a truck ran over me last night. I open my toiletry kit and take out a bottle of aspirin. I tap out two and dry-swallow.

Then I take a deep breath. I need some coffee. As I pad to the kitchenette, I notice that the coffee maker is still on. Odd. I tilt my head. I approach it and notice that there's still a cup's worth of coffee in it.

"I drank coffee?" I ask myself.

My eyes move back to the living room. There on the coffee table is a mug, and inside it's still half-filled with the mild Italian roast I like. Like a punch in the face, all the memories from last night come flooding back.

I have to hold on to the counter in order to stay upright. My knees shake from the force of my mortification. Dina and I kissed during the fireworks display.

Crap. Crap. Crap. Crap.

This is not good.

In order to distract myself before my mind implodes from the consequences of what I've done, I busy myself by making coffee. I dump out the old pot and give it a quick rinse. I add a cup or so into the reservoir. I remove the old filter, put in a new one, and place a couple of teaspoons of the Italian roast that came with our welcome basket onto it. Then I hit Start.

As the coffee brews, my hands shake. What could Dina be thinking right about now? She certainly didn't wait for me to wake up, as I'm all alone in the suite.

My phone rings. I gasp in surprise.

Thinking it might be her, I hurry to one of the couches. I pick up my phone from the coffee table and look at the screen. I breathe a sigh of relief when I see my agent's name on the screen.

"Dwight," I say after I answer the call. "I was just about to call you."

"Are you ready for tomorrow?" he asks, genuine concern in his voice. "I haven't heard from you in a couple of days."

"Just a bit busy. That's all," I say.

"Are you still in France?" He pauses. "What are you doing there, anyway?"

I rub my forehead. The aspirin's working, but not enough to ease my headache all the way. I'm still hungover. "Just taking a much-needed vacation before the big event tomorrow, that's all," I say, going with part of the truth. In this aspect of my life, I don't need lies. He will understand. "Before leaving New York, I was starting to feel some burnout. Being here is exactly what I needed to recharge."

"That's actually really good. I think this break will do you some good. Especially since we'll start the tour as soon as you get back from Edinburgh."

I close my eyes and breathe out slowly. "Thank you so much for understanding, Dwight. I really appreciate it. I'm really looking forward to tomorrow and to the tour."

"That's all I want to hear. Focus on getting ready, then call me when you get to Scotland."

I nod even though I know he can't see me. "I'll make sure to do that."

"Good. You know all I want is what's best for you, right?" Dwight asks, but I know he's not waiting for a response. "Go murder out there."

"That's the plan." I chuckle.

"I can feel many good things coming for you, Claire. It's like a shift is happening in the air for your career. Ride it like you've never ridden anything in your life."

I smile. "Goodbye, Dwight."

"Don't forget to call me, okay?"

"I won't."

I end the call just in time for my coffee to finish brewing. I stand, taking my phone with me, and walk back to the counter. I open the cupboard in front of me and take out a fresh cup.

Only then do I notice that the suite is cleaner than when we first got here. My heart squeezes. Dina cleaned up the place? I mean, I surely would have heard housekeeping, right?

I think I'm still drunk, because tears rise as I realize the complications of what it means to be with Dina and how it will affect my show. If I want us to be together, I will have to drop the Single part of my act. Dwight will not be happy about that.

I understand where he's coming from. It would mean having to rework my jokes, since I won't have the heart to deliver the old ones about me being single. I'm so screwed.

This is the first time I'm faced with the idea of choosing between having feelings for someone and my career. I don't even know if Dina feels the same way. Am I willing to sacrifice everything for the uncertainty that comes with continuing this fake relationship with her?

Yet when I think back, I know she kissed me back. And damn, she's an excellent kisser. I might be out of practice, but I believe we both enjoyed ourselves.

I receive a text. I look at my screen and tap the message icon. It's from Dina.

Okay, she doesn't completely hate me. That's a good thing. I think.

Her message is about the garden party, reminding me that it's already happening. I rack my brain and remember that it's one of the activities planned on the list the chateau gave us. With so many events going on day to day, I lost track of them all. Of course, the hangover isn't helping much either.

I fold my arms onto the counter and drop my forehead over them. I groan. Going to a garden party is the last thing I want to do right now.

I'm too overwhelmed with everything I'm feeling. I have Edinburgh tomorrow and a tour after that. There's the kiss with Dina. It's just too much.

Being with a lot of people at a party means I'll have to perform, pretend I'm Dina's doting fiancée.

My stomach flips. I have feelings for her. On my part, there won't be pretending necessary. I want to be with her. I want to hold her. I want to kiss her again.

I can already imagine what she's wearing. It's definitely going to be some pretty dress that's going to flatter her complexion and her body. I will definitely have to buy something nice in town to match her, because I wouldn't want to embarrass her. Not this time around. And the things we bought just won't do.

Yet the idea of knowing she's the one who will be pretending guts me to the bone. I don't want her to pretend. I'm at a precipice in my career, and I wish she'd at least acknowledge that fact.

She's getting a promotion because of my participation in this. Can't she show me where we're at?

Her text doesn't say anything else. Doesn't even indicate if she feels differently.

Is she doing this because she has to? Am I to be tolerated for the duration? I might as well cut my heart out now.

To face all those people at the party? Her boss. Parker. The other partners. It matters that the chateau is packed with couples. Most of them—if not all—will likely be at the party. It's another stage that I have to be on, only it's grass instead of wood.

I wonder if I can talk Dina into letting me out of going. I read through her previous texts to me. I skip the ones where she's worried because I'm not picking up.

Toward the top, one says that Bob wants Dina and I to be at the garden party because he has a surprise for us. My stomach drops. What could that be?

Yet my mind always drifts back to Dina. Is there any chance for us to be together? Am I the only one going out on a limb here? And—let's face it, because this is more likely—if she doesn't feel the same way, can I be happy knowing that?

CHAPTER TWENTY-THREE

Dina

THE GARDEN party is a splendid affair. Chateau Blanc is indeed the perfect backdrop for any event. I think that was their goal when they allowed the grounds to be transformed into something straight out of *Architectural Digest*.

I can easily imagine weddings happening here. And not just those one-day shindigs either. I'm talking about multiday affairs that involve a welcome party, a stag-and-doe party, a rehearsal dinner, picnics, you name it.

Fruit trees are scattered everywhere in this part of the garden. They have a collection of ancient apple trees, cherry trees, medlar trees, and almond trees, which are wrapped in climbing roses. They also have a section just for herbs. At the edge of the garden stands a mighty oak that isn't too tall. Instead, its branches spread out, allowing for a giant patch of shade.

Pink and white flower balls made of the most delicate rice paper hang from the branches. Hedges cut straight serve to mark the perimeter of the garden just for the fruit trees. A gazebo stands to one side with benches and climbing floral vines, and a stone fountain in the center of the entire space gurgles peacefully for the guests.

A six-piece orchestra is arranged in the gazebo. They play soft classical music in the background. Mostly Chopin.

One would think that since this is a garden party, it would look like a picnic. Oh no. It's not that kind of garden party. Yesterday was the picnic. Fun and games. And a kiss at the end. My stomach flips at the memory.

Round tables are arranged on the grass. They have elegant cream tablecloths, centerpieces made of bright spring flowers, and the most beautiful fine china that matches the pastel colors of the party. Each guest, upon arriving, is given a basket and invited to pick as much fruit from the trees as their basket can hold. This they are free to take back to their rooms with them as a kind of party favor.

There are servers dressed smartly in black bow ties and freshly ironed white shirts. They even wear gloves as they walk among the guests, brandishing silver platters filled with the finest hors d'oeuvres, from canapés made of flaky puff pastry to grilled shrimp, beef satay skewers, and cheese-and-fruit kebabs. Each one looks better than the next.

As for drinks, you have your choice of lightly alcoholic like mimosas or colorful nonalcoholic drinks like tropical teasers—basically ginger beer with Robinsons squash cordial. It's actually really good. I've already had three of them.

This party is like a waking dream. I can't believe I'm actually here. I'm wearing a butter-yellow dress with a scalloped hem and a boat neckline. It has a belt around the waist for purely ornamental value. As for shoes, I chose wedges to keep from sinking into the grass.

You know how ducks look serene as they glide across a placid lake, but their legs are moving a mile a minute underneath? That's me right now. I'm poised and professional on the outside, giving coy smiles to anyone who comes up to talk with me, while on the inside I'm freaking the fuck out.

I'm barely keeping it together. Pretty soon I might have to switch to the alcoholic stuff just to calm my fried nerves. But I'm afraid if I do that, I'll get drunk, and there's nothing pretty about that picture.

You don't want to see me sloshed; I promise. Because of the years I've spent keeping all my feelings down in the name of being the best I can be at my job, all that pent-up energy has to come out sometime, right? Well, when you get me drunk, you'll find out how ugly I can get. Pressure cookers have nothing on me.

A senior partner comes by with his wife, a pretty blond with boobs that are surely not God-given—but to each his own. He smiles at me and I smile back. His wife smiles too. She looks deep into her mimosas.

"Ms. Oliver," he says, "where is that hilarious fiancée of yours? She's just the kind of entertainment we need to kick this party up a notch."

"She's running a little late, Mr. Turner," I say, covering for Claire's absence. I really am hoping that she's just running a little late and this is not another lie that I have to tell everyone. "She's heading to Edinburgh tomorrow for the comedy festival, so she's working on some new material for her act."

"She is such a hoot," the wife says. "I got cramps during the welcome dinner when she performed."

"Susan, that's not something we say in polite company," Mr. Turner corrects.

See, this is the problem with marriages with a big age gap. The wife is clearly a trophy to be tolerated because she's a nice ornament to have. I feel sad for her.

"I'm there with you. I have to make sure that my bladder is empty when Claire is on stage," I say to save the wife from further embarrassment. "She actually has plans of shooting a special for Netflix."

"Impressive." Mr. Turner nods once. "The rest of the partners and I have been wondering why it took you so long to introduce her to us. We're all family here. I hope you don't forget that."

Before I can answer, Parker comes up beside me and puts his hands on my shoulders. "Steven, let's not put too much pressure on Dina about being family. I'm sure she knows that," he admonishes. "This day is for mingling and relaxation. Enjoy the party. Bob says there's enough time for work when we get back to New York. Now, if you'll excuse us, I have something I need to ask Dina."

He steers me away from the Turners, and when we get out of earshot, I say, "Thank you for the save. I was running out of air over there."

Parker turns around and faces me. "You're welcome. We have to stick together. Now, where's that lovely fiancée of yours?"

To think I thought I'd just dodged that bullet. I've actually been avoiding Bob for that same reason. The fewer lies I have to tell, the better.

I play it off by saying, "You know comedians. They're not supposed to be awake this time of day. Claire's more of a night owl."

"Oh, I know what you mean." Parker rolls his eyes. "I'm that way too. Sometimes when shoots run late, I stay in bed until I get my full eight hours. Wouldn't want to get those wrinkles too early."

"I completely understand. I have an eighteen-step beauty routine to prevent exactly that."

His eyes widen. "Mine is twenty steps. We have to compare notes sometime. I'd love to hear which products you use to keep that skin looking dewy and supple." He crosses his arms and pouts. "I envy all that gorgeousness."

"Says the model who's the new face of Dior," I tease.

"That billboard on Times Square is completely outrageous!" But his face says otherwise. "Now, I have to leave you because I need to check on the caterers. One of the platters has this pastry that I want to know the name of. I want to make sure I have them for the next party I plan for Bob and I."

"Let me know what you find out." I toast him.

"Tell me when that wonderful fiancée of yours arrives. Bob wants to talk to the both of you about something."

"What's the surprise? You have to tell me."

Parker raises a perfectly plucked eyebrow at me. "My lips are totally sealed. Bob will kill me if I blab. It'll be the Masino surprise party fiasco all over again."

He flits away, leaving me to wonder what Bob has up his sleeve. I put down my nonalcoholic drink and switch to a mimosa. One or two glasses won't hurt as long as I chase them with food. I can get through this.

No matter how beautiful the party is, I can't hide the fact that Claire hasn't arrived. With each minute that passes, and with each senior partner I lie about her whereabouts to, I die a little more inside. How could she do this to me?

I thought after the kiss last night that we went to bed on good terms. Sure, I snuck away early to work out some of my pent-up frustration at the gym, but surely she can't hold that against me. She was sleeping so soundly that I didn't want to wake her.

I refuse to go and get her. I'm not her mother, to go knocking on her door and yell at her to come down. Is this a pattern between us? She ghosts me each time something happens?

I'm starting to get tired of this routine. Claire says one thing, but she completely has no follow-through. And here I am, left in the lurch. Having to cover for her when she's just my fake fiancée in all of this.

By my third mimosa, I'm forced to accept the fact that I've been abandoned. It looks increasingly like Claire isn't going to show up. I'm starting to hate being in this dream and want to wake up.

Not only will I be embarrassed because she didn't show, I might have to finally come clean. This is the day I truly lose everything. I lose a possible promotion I've always wanted. And since all the senior partners are here, I might even lose the job I'm good at.

Slowly but surely, without drawing much attention to myself, I make my way to the edge of the party. I need to find a quiet, secluded place where I can escape without being seen so that I can cry. Because what else can I do?

Chapter Twenty-Four

Claire

SINCE I have nothing I want to wear to a garden party—and jeans are totally not an option since the ones I wore yesterday have grass stains on them—I make my way to the front desk and ask if I can buy something in town.

I question myself every step of the way before getting into the car with the driver they lend me. I walk into the first store I see and ask if they have anything I can wear to a garden party. When they show me the dresses, I grimace. I already know Dina will be in a dress. I originally wanted to be in a suit.

Seeing no other options at the first store, I walk into another higher-end store where things are all overpriced. I itch the entire time I'm there. It's been so long since I've paid full price for anything. In the end I just can't stand it, and I run outside to spend a few minutes on my phone looking for secondhand stores. Keenly aware that time is ticking away, I ask the driver to take me to one of them.

The nice lady at the counter there does help me. I ask if she can find a suit that I could wear for a garden party. She smiles and comes out with several selections for me.

In the end, I go with a baby blue linen suit with a tailored jacket and wide-leg pants that move when I walk. Underneath, I keep it simple with a white button-up, making sure that the top two buttons remain open. For the shoes, I go with platform espadrille sneakers that give me a couple extra inches of height.

Because the woman at the store insists, I add a hat to complete my ensemble. I look like I stole a suitcase from some crime boss from Miami. I look good, if I do say so myself.

The car picks me up from the store and we head straight back to the chateau. With each minute that passes, my urge to heave gets stronger. I've already been away too long. Dina must be beside herself with worry.

When we finally make it back, I run into Pullen and ask her to point the way. She ushers me toward the back garden. Along the way, I appreciate the giant lilies in a crystal vase on a table at the foyer. There's a double staircase beyond that leads to the rear grounds.

We go through a sitting room that might as well be taken out of a magazine, it looks so good. From the couches to the fireplace, I can only imagine one day living in a place so opulent. Chateau Blanc is truly a place of dreams.

I'm pointed toward the open French doors that lead onto a patio. There are some party guests there with drinks loitering about. I ignore them and head straight for the stone railing, my trembling hands in my pockets.

My eyes scan the party. The scene reminds me of *The Great Gatsby*, except we're not in the roaring twenties. Good thing I went with a lighter suit. Everyone is in pastels. The linen is a good choice. I should have tipped the woman at the store for her help.

I search for Dina among the people gathered. They all have drinks in their hands and are picking from trays being carried by servers. This is far from the parties I'm used to attending at comedy clubs. I feel like I'm in an episode of a soap opera.

Dina and I find each other at the same time. The instant my eyes land on her in her pretty yellow dress, she looks up to where I'm standing. Looking at the smile she gives me is like witnessing the sun rise for the first time. It lights up my whole world.

What I've done to deserve that smile escapes me. In the back of my mind, I'm glad that I came, for that smile alone. It's like I hung the moon and the stars for her.

I nod at her in greeting. She excuses herself from the conversation she's currently in the middle of while I make my way to the side steps that will take me to the garden proper. She meets me at the bottom of the steps.

"You came," she says, breathless.

"Of course I did," I say, giving her a kiss on the cheek. Inside I feel a click like a piece snapping into place. "I'm sorry for being late. I had to go shopping."

"I can see that." Her grin is positively mischievous.

"Don't you dare take credit for this suit I'm wearing," I tease.

The tailored jacket is formfitting, as Dina would have advised, but I do have some fashion sense on my own also.

"You're welcome," she teases me right back.

She's definitely taking credit for the way I'm dressed. I don't mind. I did think about the occasion, so it's really more for her than for anything else.

I take her hand in mine and kiss the top of it.

"Get ready," she whispers. "We're about to be descended upon by the hounds."

"As long as you're by my side, I'll be fine."

Dina preens. She has her hair up, which accentuates the length of her neck, and I take a sense of pride in the fact that I'm with the most beautiful woman at this party.

Bob and Parker are the first to come near us. Parker beams as he gives me a kiss on both cheeks. Bob does the same, smiling so wide I'm almost afraid his cheeks will crack.

"You finally made it," he says.

"I apologize for being late," I reply. "Thank you for keeping my fiancée company."

"Well, you're here now," Parker says. "We can finally start talking about that surprise, which involves taking photos, by the way."

I nod, pretending I know what he's talking about. Dina leans in and whispers that she has no idea what's going on. I brace for impact.

One after the other, the senior partners and their wives greet us and make small talk. It finally dawns on me that we're the only gay couple besides Bob and Parker at this party. Among the senior partnership, that is.

"That's what Bob's working on changing," Dina explains to me as I pick up one of the colorful drinks from a passing tray.

I take a sip and enjoy the sweetness. "There's no alcohol in here, right?"

Dina nods. "Thank you for coming."

"Thank you for helping me win that bet yesterday," I say back. "It's a total lifesaver."

A pretty pink blush brings color to her cheeks. A few more couples from other agencies come by and introduce themselves. I feel like the entire party wants to meet up. Through the ordeal—because it *is* an ordeal trying to remember their names—I hold on to Dina's hand. She doesn't move to let go, which I take as a great sign.

Once in a while, when there's a break between meeting people, I pick up an hors d'oeuvre and pop it into my mouth. Meeting people makes me hungry. I'm used to smiling and shaking hands, since at my shows there are usually meet-and-greets afterward. People pay extra for those, of course. Here I'm doing it for free.

When I feel like I've met everyone besides the servers, I relax a little. Now we can hang back and enjoy the party. Or so I think until someone yells for a show.

Bob makes his way toward us and smiles at me. "Yes, Claire. Will you give us a peek at the comedy set you have planned for the festival since we can't be there?"

"Oh!" Parker claps in excitement. "Please? That means I don't have to sneak away just to go and watch you."

My face glows bright red. I'm sure of it, because I'm suddenly sweating through the shirt under my jacket. Now, hopefully my jacket is thick enough to hide the evidence of my mounting anxiety.

"You don't have to do it if you don't want to," Dina whispers to me discreetly. "Just say the word and I will deflect so hard they will not see me coming."

But by then the guests at the party are all chanting for me to take the stage. Since there isn't a real stage, I think they mean the gazebo where the orchestra has currently stopped playing. Declining doesn't even come to mind. I'll take any chance to perform.

"I got this," I whisper back.

"You sure?" Her worry touches me.

I bring her hand to my lips and kiss the top. She smiles and gives me a reassuring squeeze. What I did before I met her, I don't remember anymore.

As much as I don't want to, I let go of her hand and make my way to the gazebo. "Take a break, boys," I tell them with a wobbly grin, and they leave their instruments.

It's only been a few days since I've been on stage and I already feel rusty as hell. The butterflies in my stomach are bumping around. Instead of solid ground, I feel like I'm at sea.

Some helpful person actually hands me a mic. I don't know where it came from. I clear my throat and the mic picks it up.

"At least we know this works," I say, already getting a laugh from the gathering guests.

Dina stands with Bob and Parker. I look to her and she nods at me in encouragement. A zing of excitement goes through me.

I bring the mic to my mouth and say, "Honey, I'm about to say things from my single days. Please don't call off the engagement after this."

The crowd erupts in laughter as Dina blows me a kiss.

CHAPTER TWENTY-FIVE

Dina

I STAND in awe of Claire. I've seen her show many times, but she's really on a whole different level today. You see her switch from regular person to comedian in seconds.

There's something about watching her. She's a natural performer. I can't see her doing anything else. If the reaction of the crowd today is any indication, she's definitely going a long way. We need people like her in the world.

You'd think such an uptight crowd wouldn't enjoy Claire's humor, but based on the roaring laughter around us, they love her. Parker is practically crying beside me as he watches. Even the women with faces pumped full of Botox are cracking their contours from laughing.

Bob takes a little longer to get on the wagon with everyone else. He starts off as reserved. Eventually Claire gets him with her dutch oven joke and the perils of sharing a bed with someone. Who knew my boss appreciated toilet humor?

"I dated a girl once who didn't eat bread," Claire says. She looks at the crowd. "I know some of you ladies here are like that. You have that 'I haven't touched a carb in years' look about you."

They laugh, even though Claire hit the nail on the head. I definitely noticed not all of women were enjoying the puff pastry hors d'oeuvres. Some of them just eat a shrimp or two and guzzle mimosas like there's no tomorrow.

Even the servers can't hold straight faces as they pass with food and drinks. There's one guy who I thought would drop the tiger prawns on his platter because he snorted a little too hard. I realize that's the magic of Claire. No matter who's in the crowd, she's able to capture their attention and hold it.

She even makes the older senior partners laugh with her brand of humor. As soon as she hits that punch line, they're slapping their thighs.

Even though I've heard some of these jokes already, I'm still laughing. Claire puts a new spin to them every time.

Sometimes she even works the crowd. She'll pick someone out because of the way they look or the way they dress and incorporate them into the joke. Nothing offensive. Everyone's a great sport about it.

"She's amazing," Bob tells me as he leans close.

His booming laughter is a reward to my ears. It's nice to see him enjoying himself, since most of the time he's so serious when he's at the office.

"Don't I know it," I say without taking my eyes off Claire.

I stand there like a proud fiancée. I'm taking ownership of the moment. Once in a while Claire will look my way and give me a smile or a wink. My heart flutters every time.

Is this what it feels like to date a rock star? I feel so hot and bothered, but I stifle the urge to fan myself. Claire is a celebrity in her own right. I even see the way some of the women are looking at her. They are lusting after my girl.

The instant that thought hits my head, I know. I want Claire to be my girl. I can't stand the idea of someone else having her. She needs to be in my life or I won't be able to call it a life at all.

How did I live before I met her? I certainly didn't laugh this much or this hard. She's brought out a side of me that I never thought I had.

The harder the crowd laughs, the more Claire revs up her performance. It's like she's feeding off the energy that's being sent her way. She's quick to respond and delivers each joke like she's shooting a gun. She's a sniper up there.

Now I understand what she meant about murdering. She's killing with her humor. Her mouth the gun. Her jokes the bullets.

A part of me wonders if Claire really dated all these girls she mentions. The one that doesn't eat bread. The one with the online shopping addiction. They all seem like characters, but they also seem so real based on the way she tells the stories.

I have to admit, I find myself a little jealous that she's been with these women, fictional or not. I want her to be all mine.

I gasp when I realize I might be falling in love with the woman performing up there in the gazebo. When I saw her at the veranda looking down at the party? I felt my heart jump to my throat.

One, because I couldn't believe she actually came. I'd actually lost all hope of her showing up. I was prepared to call it quits.

But like a goddess appearing out of nowhere, there she stood in a light blue suit that set off her hair and complexion. I've never lusted after anyone more than I've lusted after her. She actually went out and bought herself a suit for this party. If that isn't love, I don't know what is.

I'm not one for hats because they always made my head look too big, but on Claire? She makes the accessory seem natural and sexy. I can actually feel my heart wanting to punch a hole in my chest, that's how hard it's beating.

Then, when she placed a kiss on my cheek? How I wanted it to be on my lips! I actually barely hid a pout; I was that upset. Then she kissed the top of my hand, and just like that all was right with the world.

If you think about it, I have every right to be upset with her. I could have been screaming at her in anger, but there's something about being in Claire's presence that immediately calms me. I've never felt more secure with who I am than when I'm with her.

I'd like to think that when she kissed me at the lake yesterday, it wasn't just the excitement and the romantic atmosphere talking. How can I not reward that devotion with a reciprocation of her feelings?

Claire makes me want to open myself up to the possibility of being with someone after years of staying single. Of putting my career above being in a relationship. She's so wonderful that I would be a fool to let her go. She has her moments, sure, but that pales in comparison to what she has to offer.

"You're lucky to have her in your life," Parker says, as if he can hear the thoughts running around in my head.

"I actually am," I say, meaning it.

"Speaking of lucky," Bob says, "I'd like to talk to you about a potential partnership at the agency. Assuming that's something you're open to discussing?"

I gasp. I almost forgot about that. Bob waits for a response, but my throat closes in my excitement. This is it. It's finally happening. The most I can do in that moment is nod.

He smiles. "Good. We'll set the meeting for tomorrow afternoon."

"Thank you," I squeak out after clearing my throat.

"No need to thank me." He pats me on the shoulder. "It's well-deserved."

Claire ends her show to the loudest applause I've ever heard. Some of the men even whistle their appreciation. Claire bows, a huge smile on her face.

She says something about being here all night and tipping the waiters. It has to be some inside joke, because a few of the men laugh like they know what she means. I for one don't care if I don't understand what she's saying in that moment. All I care about is her face is glowing and that she's happy.

Claire tells the band that they can go back to playing now. Then she steps down from the gazebo and returns to my side. I take her face in my hands and give her a kiss.

She's shocked at first but quickly melts into the moment. We part as people applaud and cheer that too. I look into her eyes and make my decision. I'm going to tell her my feelings tonight. There's no point in waiting any longer.

"That was amazing," Parker says, practically jumping out of his skin.

"Thank you for that, Claire," Bob says, shaking her hand. "Brilliant. I look forward to seeing your future Netflix special."

Claire merely smiles as she takes my hand in hers again. I give her a squeeze, and she looks up at me. I wink.

"Now that I've got the both of you here, I'd like to discuss with you the surprise I have planned." Bob glances at Parker, who comes closer to him.

"Actually, I was the one who suggested it," Parker says. "Don't take all the credit."

Bob chuckles. "It's a great suggestion."

"What is it?" Claire asks, looking from me to Bob to Parker.

"You tell them." Bob nudges Parker, who seems ready to burst.

He clasps his hands together and says, "Since we're already at one of the most romantic places in the world and you two are already affianced, why don't we have your wedding here?"

All of Parker's words fly over my head as my skin grows cold.

"What?" Claire asks, surprise clear in that one word.

"A wedding!" Parker repeats. "We can have it here after you return from Edinburgh."

"Chateau Blanc has already graciously agreed," Bob explains. "In return, all they want are the rights to the pictures for their website and their brochures. They want to branch out and make this place a wedding destination as well."

"Since you two are already the perfect couple, they jumped at the chance!" Parker adds.

I no longer feel the solid ground beneath my feet. My heart stops.

CHAPTER TWENTY-SIX

Claire

STILL RIDING high on my performance, I don't know what to say about the wedding ambush Bob and Parker just sprung on us. Dina hasn't said a word at all either. How did I go from talking about the women I've dated to about to marry the woman I'm fake engaged to?

Parker whisks Dina and I away to some corner of the chateau's magnificent garden for those photos he said we would be taking. Bob and the big man of Chateau Blanc are there the entire time, supervising. We take posed shots, candid shots, we even take a few looking into each other's eyes as if we were figurines on a wedding cake.

I keep looking to Dina for some guidance about what's happening. She doesn't say anything to me. She just poses each time the photographer asks us to change things up.

The longer she takes to say something, the more confused I am about this entire situation we find ourselves in. Are we seriously getting married?

After the party, Dina and I walk back to our suite.

As a way to alleviate some of my nervous energy, I say, "What did you think about my performance? I think there are still a few things I can tweak. Maybe I should remove my sleepwalking girlfriend bit and replace it with something else. Then again, maybe it's too late? I really don't know."

"Right, too late," she says, her voice sounding far away.

Unwilling to bring up the bomb Bob dropped on us, I keep going. "Then again, I can always go with my usual jokes. I mean, I know those from the bottom of my heart. The crowd at the comedy festival will all be new, so I'd think that they'd be the best source for fresh reactions. But do I really want to stay with the old when I can bring in new stuff? Do I take the risk, or should I play it safe?"

I'm talking so fast that I'm running out of breath.

"Play it safe, right," Dina responds, yet I don't think she's really responding to me.

I never thought this would happen, but I don't know what else to say. There is a huge elephant between us, and I'm not sure if I should be the first one to bring attention to it or if I should wait for Dina to say something. Is this something she wants? The bigger question is: is this something I want? It's so sudden. I'm freaking out.

"We need to talk," Dina finally says after she closes the door behind us.

"Thank God!" I say in relief, standing in the middle of the living room. "I honestly don't know what happened back there. Did we just get highjacked into getting married?"

Her lips grow thin. "You should leave for Edinburgh tonight."

"What?" My heart slams into my throat. "Don't you want to talk about the wedding? I mean, it's going to happen when I get back, so we need a plan."

"I already have a plan," she says, flat and without emotion. "I'm going to rebook all the travel and hotel accommodations you'll need to go from here to Edinburgh and from there back to New York."

"I don't understand."

"Claire, I'm not going to marry you."

"What?" All the blood in my body drops to the pads of my feet. I'm surprised I can even remain standing. "But what about your promotion? Won't backing out of the wedding cost you that?"

"How do you honestly see this playing out?" Dina challenges. "We get married, I get my promotion, then we get a divorce?"

"We planned on breaking up after this anyway, so what's the difference?"

In all honesty, I don't know why I'm defending our situation. Dina is giving me the out that I need. Am I really willing to get married to someone I'm just starting to have feelings for? What would that mean for my career?

"I'm not willing to subject you to marriage, Claire. This situation has gone too far." A frown pulls down the corners of Dina's lips. "Getting married is a serious deal, and I for one don't want to get divorced. As much as my parents had their hang-ups, they're still together to this day. I'd like to have that for myself one day. A fake relationship, I can put up with. A fake wedding? A fake marriage? That's where I draw the line."

"Wow!" I feel my temper rising. "Good to know where I stand with you on this. Apparently I'm just fake relationship material. That will make a great joke on stage one day."

"Claire." Dina's shoulders drop. "You know I didn't mean it that way."

"Oh yeah? Then how did you mean it? Because from where I'm standing, your words are pretty clear."

"Can't you see that I'm doing us both a favor here? Can you honestly say that you want to be married to me?"

"Just admit it." I shake my head. "You just don't want to be with someone like me. This is all a sham to you."

"Don't sell yourself short. You're attractive as fuck."

"Uhm… thanks?" My face suddenly goes hot. "That honestly does not sound like a compliment right now. I'd rather you slap me."

The air between us shifts. There's a seriousness that I can no longer avoid. She might as well know so that it's all out in the open.

"You know what?" I make up my mind. "You're right."

"What?" A look of devastation crosses her features, but she quickly covers it with a calm mask. "So you're agreeing to this?"

"I neglected to tell you that my agent wants me to go on a national tour after Edinburgh," I say as quickly as I can. Like ripping off the Band-Aid. Since we're already making big decisions, adding one more won't matter much in the grand scheme of things.

"That's amazing," she says, a little too breathless.

"He says the news of me performing at the comedy festival is gaining traction. That theaters want to book me."

"That's totally a big deal, isn't it?"

I nod. In the back of my mind, I'm happy she actually remembers the time I told her about what it meant to move up from clubs to theaters. About how much exposure that will get for me. That's the thing that's so special about Dina—the thing I truly appreciate. She makes me feel seen, which makes this situation all the more painful.

"He's excited, and quite frankly, I'm excited too. This tour will mean a lot for my career, and being married to someone isn't exactly going to make that any easier. Being single is part of my act, after all."

"Right." Dina can't hide the hurt on her face fast enough.

"So yeah," I continue while my chest crumbles. "It's a good idea to fly back to New York after Edinburgh. What about your promotion, though?"

I have to ask, because that's what started all of this in the first place.

Dina tilts her head in confusion. "Why are you still worried about that?"

"Okay, it looks like you're not worried about it." But something inside me breaks. Did we do all of this for nothing?

"I'll take care of it," she says. "Why don't you just worry about your act? Go back to your brand."

In this, she's totally right. "I'm known for being fun, fat, and single. I know, I'm not fat, but that's part of the shtick, so roll with me here."

She closes her mouth, swallowing the contradiction I know she was about to let out. It's nice to have someone who believes otherwise and is willing to defend you for it. Unfortunately, that might be an act too.

"You have your life and I have mine," she finally says.

"Exactly!" A part of me is glad she understands what I'm telling her. The other part of me is sad that she understands what I'm telling her. "When I leave, we go back to our lives and maybe just stay friends."

"I think it'll be better if we cut off contact entirely," she says, which is a dagger to my heart. "We can't have people getting suspicious. If we remain friends, we'll just send Bob and your audience the wrong message."

I'm taken aback by her words. I know I'm the one who initiated this part of the conversation, but I honestly don't like where it's going.

But maybe she's right. What's the point of remaining friends?

Not wanting to prolong the awkward air that suddenly formed between us, I say, "I'll start packing my bags."

She moves toward the suite door. "And I'll start making the arrangements at the chateau's business center. I'll leave all the details with the concierge. The car will be waiting for you outside the chateau when you're done."

I turn and head straight into the room we've shared for several nights now. Her things and my things mingle together. I swipe at the first tear that falls as soon as my hand touches my bag.

CHAPTER TWENTY-SEVEN

Dina

IN THE span of a conversation, everything in my life imploded. I was so happy during the latter half of the garden party. Claire was happy too. Then Bob and Parker ruined everything with a single surprise.

Before that, I was willing to see how things might progress with Claire. Take things to the next level. Bob and Parker want us to take it to the *ultimate* level. Knowing Claire—and ultimately, myself—we're not ready for marriage. Fake relationship or not.

I had it all planned out too. After the party, I'd swipe a bottle of the best champagne at the bar, take her back to our suite, and celebrate our successes: for her, the act she'd perform in Edinburgh, and for me, signing the promotion contract. Then we'd see where the night took us.

All that went to hell in a handbasket. I find myself booking all her travel and accommodations and calling the front desk about a car to take her to the station. When I return to the room, I hold on to hope that she'll still be there. Why? I don't know. All her things are gone. As if she was never there in the first place.

When I close the door to what was once our suite, a door to my heart closes too. In that moment, the honeymoon suite seems too big. Too empty. For just myself and my broken heart.

I sit on one of the ridiculously expensive couches for about an hour just staring into space after she leaves. Suddenly I don't remember how to move. I forget how to speak.

I've ended relationships before. I've been broken up with and I've been the one doing the breaking up. None of them felt half as devastating as this one. It's like my world upturned and I don't know which side is right.

My thoughts are so jumbled, I can't even think straight. I'm really not seeing anything. I just stare and stare until my eyes go dry.

When I finally remember how to move, I pick myself up. My body moves as if from memory. I'm not in full command. I remove my dress and let it sink to the floor. Then I step into the bathroom and straight into the shower. No more going out for me tonight.

A numbness spreads all over me like the water raining down from the showerhead. Is this what getting hit by a car is like? You don't register the pain right away. You're just there, in shock, thinking, *I got hit by a car.* Only when you see a bone sticking out do you register the pain

I fiddle with the controls until the water is scalding hot. It doesn't drive away the cold lump that's formed inside me. I pick up a sponge, squeeze some soap onto it, and close my fist around it until bubbles come out. Then I start rubbing my arms until my skin lathers.

I must have rubbed too hard, because it starts to hurt, but it's not as painful as what I feel beneath the surface. I stop before I rub myself raw anyway.

There is soap. There is steam. The tears I didn't think I possessed drip from my eyes to mix with the water that's now running clear. All the soap is gone. Now it's just water and my tears together until you can't tell one from the other.

I turn off the shower and put my back against the wall. I slide to the floor. My legs are no longer able to support my weight. They stretch out before me. My arms lie wilted on each side of me.

I drop my head and let my tears fall freely until they pool on my thighs. My tears are silent. I make no sound. That's always been the case since I was small.

My mother abhorred crying. She said it wasn't something strong girls did. They never showed their emotions. So when I cried, it was always in secret. Inside my closet. In the shower. I got really good at silent crying.

I can't believe how foolish I've been. I thought that just because I acknowledged my feelings for someone that everything would be all right. That I would tell her how I feel and she would accept me and everything would come together like it's supposed to.

Like in the movies. The guy meets the girl. They fall in love. They tell each other that they love each other, and poof! Happily ever after.

What they don't tell you is that movies are not mirrors of real life. In real life, a wrench always gets thrown in and destroys the working mechanisms of the engine that's supposed to be running smoothly. It's always when you least expect it, too.

So here you are, crying on the floor. All alone in the honeymoon suite. It's supposed to be the most romantic place in the world. Instead, it's where heartache happens.

I lift my head until it bumps against the marble behind me. There's a thump, but I don't feel anything. The rending in my chest is much more painful. Much more intense.

I've already been telling myself that Claire has a life of her own. I merely pulled her into mine. It's no wonder she wants to return to that life after all this. I should accept the consequences as they are.

Claire was happy before I came along. Before I presented her with this scheme of mine. Out of the goodness of her heart, she agreed to help me.

Now she has what she wanted and my career is in jeopardy. Maybe it wasn't meant to be in the first place, since I've been lying this whole time. It's not her fault that she wants to take care of herself. She's worked too hard at her career to sacrifice it all for someone like me.

If there's someone to blame, it's myself. I let myself get caught up in my emotions. Claire is just living her life. Taking time out to help me. I'm the one who's been expecting more when I should have had my guard up.

Now I'm the loser sitting sprawled out in the shower crying my eyes out. What would my mother think if she saw me? Oh, I know— she'd say, "Dina, you do not let anyone get in the way of your ambition. Strong girls don't let others make them cry."

For once, my mother is right. I lift my hand to my face and wipe away my tears by swiping the back of it over my cheeks. At least, after all of this, maybe Bob will forgive me if I come clean. Maybe I can still keep the job I'm good at.

That's what I tell myself. So why should I be crying because of a woman who only wants to live her own life? A life I'm not a part of.

A pinch enters my heart at that last thought. I push it away. No. I shouldn't let it affect me. This is for the best.

I plant my hands on the floor and bend my knees. Using the wall behind me as leverage, I push up from the ground. I have some cleaning to do.

I dry myself with a towel. Afterward, I focus on my nightly routine. I cleanse my face and moisturize my skin. No need for mascara or lip gloss this time around. No need to look extra pretty and perfect. No one is there to see anyway.

Once I'm dressed for bed, I remove the excess pillows from the mattress and pull back the covers.

Normally I'd read a couple of chapters before going to sleep, but for once I'm too tired to stare at someone else's words. I get into bed, turn off the bedside lamp, and throw the covers over me.

When I'm comfortable, I stare at the ceiling. There's a full moon out, so the moonlight streams in like silver sunlight, allowing me to see the molding along the ceiling. It's pretty. I concentrate on my breathing.

As I reach a meditative state, I make a solemn vow not to open myself up like that again. I no longer need to put myself out there. I'm too precious to be put in such a painful situation ever again.

One brick at a time. I build an even stronger, higher wall around my heart. I need to make sure it holds and stays so that it will no longer crumble under the onslaught of someone else's attack. I apply the thickest mortar I can imagine.

As I finish building my wall of protection, I tell myself that this will be the last time I ever risk getting hurt. I will no longer allow myself to get to know someone who will break my wall. There's no need for me to be in a relationship.

All I have is myself. I've done well all these years without someone else by my side. Who's to say I will not continue to do well? At least now I have something more to look forward to.

Tomorrow, I face Bob and whatever else might happen after that.

CHAPTER TWENTY-EIGHT

Claire

AFTER A long and way-too-quiet car ride to the station, it takes two trains to get me to Edinburgh. Two hours by car and seven hours by train. That's how long I go without talking to anyone. A personal record, really.

Even when I'm deep into writing jokes, I take breaks and catch up on calls or go for lunch at my favorite diner. There's always someone to talk to. This is the first time I've been alone with my thoughts for such a hell of a long time.

And what do I think about? Dina.

I go from really pissed that she can just throw me aside like that to worried about what might happen to her job to sad that we had to leave things the way we did. Believe me, there are moments during my very long trip that I want to say screw it to my career, turn around, and marry Dina if it means she gets to keep the job she loves and we get to be together. We can figure shit out along the way.

Comedy will always be there. Opportunities will still come. But what happens when I show up at the suite, profess my love, and she turns me away again? Not only would I lose a chance at furthering my career, but I'd also break my heart for the second time in the process.

Once is enough, thank you very much.

I check into my hotel and leave my stuff in my room. I want to scope out the festival before my set tonight. I'll just catch a nap a few hours before. I'm too wired to rest.

Then my phone rings. I see Dwight's name on the screen. The last thing I want is to talk to him right now, but I did promise I'd give him a call once I got here. He just happened to beat me to it.

"Hey, Dwight," I say once I pick up the phone.

"Where are you right now?" he asks, no preamble to the conversation.

"What do you mean? I'm outside my hotel in Edinburgh."

"Good. Meet me at the Stratton Café," he says. "We need to talk strategy."

"You're in Scotland?" I blurt out, my surprise infinite.

"Just get here already."

He hangs up and I stare at the screen of my phone for the longest second. Then I ask for directions to the café he named. I didn't expect that Dwight would fly out here. Then again, it makes sense. He does love to have a plan. Like someone else I know.

Dina's face comes to mind, and my heart shrinks a couple of sizes. If I leave now, I can be back at the chateau before sunrise. Instead, I stuff my hands into my jacket pockets—the jacket she gave me—and turn toward the direction of the café.

A couple of blocks later, I walk into the café determined to make sure we smooth out all the logistics for when I return to New York so we can hit the ground running. Dwight's at a table already with his laptop open. He has a coffee beside him. I make my order at the counter and point at the table where I'll be sitting.

"Look at you," I say, approaching him. "What a sight for sore eyes."

He finishes reading something before he looks up and smiles. Okay. It looks like he's in a good mood despite the jet lag I'm sure he's feeling. That's good.

"Take a seat," he says, gesturing me over, then pointing at the chair. "Did you already place your order for something?"

"Yup. Got my coffee on the way," I say as I sit. "I honestly didn't expect to see you here, but I'm glad that you are."

"With everything happening, I didn't think this could wait. There are some things we need to talk about."

"Okay." I rub my hands together. "I'm ready."

"That's what I like to hear. Do you want the good news first or the bad news?"

"Is there really a choice? I want the good news first." It's to soften the blow for when the bad news comes. Hopefully it has nothing to do with the tour or anything related to it. The last thing I want is to create bad blood between me and the clubs I play at.

"Okay, the good news is, the theaters are starting to sell tickets, and sales are looking good," he says. "From the looks of things, depending on how your set goes tonight, you'll sell out faster than expected."

"Oh, thank God." I clutch my chest for a second. "So all I have to do is murder tonight. That's doable."

"Yes." He nods. "Your work at the clubs is paying off."

"The owners at the clubs aren't mad that I'm moving on to theaters?" I ask, almost on the verge of tears at the relief I feel. At least something is going my way.

"Not at all. What made you think they would be mad at you?"

"I don't know." I squeeze the back of my neck. "Maybe because they gave me my start and leaving them feels like a betrayal?"

"Claire, the clubs understand when a comedian needs to spread their wings. Moving up to theaters is a natural progression for your career. If that didn't happen then we'd have bigger problems to be figuring out."

"Woah!" My eyebrows shoot up to my hairline. "Okay, talk about pressure."

"I honestly think you can handle it." Dwight grins. "I wouldn't be representing you if I didn't know you'd be able to make it in the industry."

"Thanks for the vote of confidence."

"Now, as long as everything goes well tonight, you're good to go."

"Can you send me the schedule of the tour? I want to see the dates and cities."

"It's already in your inbox."

"Thank you." I've never been happier to hear those words. Then I brace myself for what's to come next. "And the bad news?"

Dwight sits back in his chair and tents his fingers together. He regards me with a serious stare. I wait for what he has to say, my heart in my throat the entire time.

"This is more like a warning than actual bad news," he begins, sounding ominous. "This will only become bad news if you don't heed my warning. Do you understand?"

I swallow and nod.

"Remember, Claire, that you are quite popular. And that popularity came from the show you've put together over the years. People respond to what you do on that stage."

"I understand."

"Do you? Okay. Then no matter what happens moving forward, regardless of any changes in your relationship status, always keep in mind the future of your show."

I feel all the blood in my body sink to the soles of my feet. I'm having a hard time getting the air my lungs need to breathe. My head is suddenly fuzzy.

Dwight and I look at each other for the longest time. It's as if he knows more than he is letting on. Has he seen the pictures? Surely not, or he would have brought them up by now.

The silence extends itself when my coffee arrives. I take several sips of the hot brew, not waiting for the thing to cool down. Maybe I'm hoping it burns my throat, giving me a way out of answering. But, then, if I can't speak now, I won't be able to perform later.

When it's clear he's waiting for confirmation from me, I say, "I'll make sure to keep that in mind."

"I trust you to do the right thing, Claire," he says. Then he stands up and reaches out a hand.

I stand as well and shake hands with him. "You won't be disappointed, Dwight."

"I'll finish up some more work here. I'm pretty sure you're itching to scope out the festival. I'll see you during your set later."

"You know me too well." When I smile, my lips wobble. "Coffee is on you."

"It's the least I can do for my rising star client."

At what cost? I ask myself. My smile fades.

It's a good thing Dwight doesn't notice. I leave the café feeling more confused than ever. I don't know what to do. This is all so fucked-up.

My stomach is in knots. It's like I narrowly escaped the firing squad in there. I step out onto the street and take the biggest deep breath I can physically hold in my lungs.

When I exhale, I remind myself that this festival is coming at the right time. I want to stop thinking about everything else for a minute and spend some time getting my head right for tonight.

I'm about to hail a cab at the sidewalk after I exit the building when my phone rings. I fish it out of my back pocket and see Dina's name on the screen. My stomach drops like I'm riding a roller coaster. At first I debate whether to pick up. Eventually, because this is Dina we're talking about, I answer.

"Hey," I say, cautious. "What's up?"

"I just wanted to make sure that you got to Edinburgh all right," Dina says, voice uncertain as well.

I hate how awkward we're being with each other. Maybe it was a bad idea to answer the call. She was the one who said we shouldn't be friends after this.

"Well, I got here."

"Good," she says.

There's a long pause afterward. I check the phone's screen. It says the call is still connected.

Okay. Odd. I would think that Dina would only call because she had something she wanted to tell me.

I'm about to ask her when she says, "Actually, the reason why I called is because Bob asked me to meet him at one of the offices here at the chateau."

"Isn't that a good thing?" I ask.

"He's going to ask me to sign the promotion contract. He told me about it yesterday at the garden party."

Ah, the infamous garden party. We were happy one second. The next we're parting ways. A part of me wishes I never went. Then maybe Dina and I wouldn't be in this situation.

Knowing she's waiting for a response from me, I say, "Congratulations. I know that's everything that you wanted. If he asks, tell him we're still together. Then after you sign, wait a couple of days and then tell him we broke up."

"I'm not going to do that."

"What? Why not?"

"I decided last night that I'm going to tell him everything."

My heart skips a beat. "But what if he fires you for it?"

"Then I'll have to find another job. I have some savings that can tide me over."

"But that's for your travel fund." A lump forms in my throat.

"I can always build it back up again. Don't worry about it. I got myself into this mess, and I will get myself out."

She says it as if it's as simple as that. Yet I know from the tone of her voice that it's anything but. I know she will be devastated if Bob fires her.

"What do you want me to do?" I ask impulsively.

In the back of my mind, I know that if she asks me to return to the chateau, I will. Was this what Dwight meant about keeping my future in mind? Am I really willing to throw everything away for Dina?

"Just break a leg out there, okay?" she says. "At least one of us has to get to live out their dreams."

She ends the call, and I stare at my phone screen, bewildered and broken. What just happened? I feel like I just got steamrolled or something.

Not once did I ever think that Dina would fall on her sword like that. She was the one to come up with the fake fiancée idea. She was the one who brought me to France and, by extension, Edinburgh.

Unsure of myself for the first time in a long while, I force myself to focus on figuring out the lay of the land at the festival. As heartbroken as I am about Dina's situation, I acknowledge that she's right. I'm already here. I might as well make the most of it.

I'll figure out the rest afterward.

CHAPTER TWENTY-NINE

Dina

ALL DAY, I count down the hours until my meeting with Bob. I don't leave the suite at all, taking advantage of the free room service. I figure if this is going to be my last chance to enjoy a place like this, I might as well get all the perks while I still can.

Then, because all they have on the TV is romantic movies, I busy myself packing my bags. I expect that after what I have to say to Bob, he'll want me to leave the premises immediately. Then, in the middle of folding my clothes so they don't wrinkle inside my luggage, I pick up my phone and call Claire.

It's an impulse I can't control. I don't even think she will pick up. But then she does, and I hate the flutter that still happens in my chest the second I hear her voice.

As expected, the call goes horribly. Awkward and painful. At least I get to wish her luck for her performance tonight. She certainly deserves to be there.

Then the phone to the suite rings. I pick it up and the concierge at the other end informs me that Bob is waiting for me at the main office of the chateau. Apparently the owner has been gracious enough to lend it to him for this purpose.

As soon as I put down the phone, I leave the suite and make my way to the office. I see no point in delaying the inevitable. Like I told Claire, I've made up my mind. There's no backing out now.

I put myself in this position. Now it's time to accept the consequences.

"Stop fidgeting," I whisper to myself when I realize I've been wringing my hands.

Along the way, I need to ask for directions. One of the staff is kind enough to escort me. I stop at the door and run my hands down the front of my dress. One, to make sure there aren't any wrinkles. And two, to wipe away any sweat that has accumulated on my palms.

"Bob?" I ask as I knock and open the door.

"Come in," he says, voice cheerful.

He's in a good mood. I bite the inside of my cheek. I hate to ruin that good humor with what I'm about to say.

"I wanted to talk to you about something." I walk in to find him standing behind a magnificent desk. The wood carving detail speaks of a bygone opulence that doesn't show in all the modern furnishings of today. In fact, the entire office holds a regal air befitting a chateau and the kings of old that used it.

"I'm so excited about this," he says, pushing the contract forward. "I believe you'll be an even bigger asset to the agency as a partner. The other partners think so too."

"That's actually what I want to talk to you about." I stop at the other side of the desk and look down at the contract. My eyes glance through the first page; then I continue flipping from the second to the next. The entire thing outlines my new responsibilities, the perks that come with those responsibilities—lots and lots of travel—and my salary. Oh boy. A slow whistle comes out of me.

"So many zeros after that five," I whisper under my breath.

That's when shit gets real for me. I swallow as my throat closes.

Bob hands over a pen. "Well, what are you waiting for?"

I shake my head, refusing the pen. "That's what I wanted to talk to you about."

The frown on Bob's face comes from a place of concern. "Is something the matter? Are you not satisfied with the terms? Because we still have a little wiggle room if you want to renegotiate."

"It's not that." I blink in an attempt to fight back the oncoming tears.

I want to get through this as professionally as I can. There's no room for crying in this moment. I take a deep breath and, on the exhale, push the contract back toward him.

"I don't understand," he says, growing serious. As if I'd slapped him in the face.

I might as well have when I say, "There's no easy way to say this."

"Then I think we should both be sitting down." He takes a seat on the oxblood leather chair behind him and points at the chair behind me.

At first, the thought of refusing to sit crosses my mind, but with how hard my knees are shaking, I can't remain upright anymore. I step back and allow the chair to catch me as I fall.

"All right," he says. "What's this you want to tell me?"

"I've been lying to you this entire time," I blurt out. I see no point in delaying any longer than I already have.

"Lying in what way?"

"You have to understand that being a partner at the agency and getting to travel the world is all I've ever wanted."

"Yet you refuse to sign the contract."

"That's because it would be wrong of me to do so."

"Why is that?"

"Because Claire isn't really my fiancée."

There. I said it. The truth is out there for all to see. Why don't I feel as liberated as I should? I'm still as stuck as a stone on the ground.

Bob narrows his gaze at me. "I don't understand."

"I knew that to get this partnership, I needed a partner of my own."

"What gave you the impression that you needed to be in a relationship to be a partner at the agency?" His frown deepens.

"Every one of the partners is married."

"Is that why you said you had a fiancée when we were at Bar Rafael?"

I nod. "So when you asked me to bring mine along, I had to find a way. That's when I met Claire."

"How did you get her to play along?"

I sigh. "I offered to get her into the Edinburgh Comedy Festival. I used my contacts in Scotland."

"Ah." Bob's eyebrows go up as if he just figured out a piece of the puzzle. "Why are you telling me this now? You could have signed the contract, become a partner, and broken up with Claire afterward."

A sad chuckle leaps out of me. "That's exactly what Claire said."

"Then why didn't you?"

"Because I couldn't see the lie through anymore." My shoulders slump.

"Does this have something to do with the wedding that Parker and I sprung on the both of you?"

"Part of it, yes." I look him in the eyes. "I couldn't drag her in deeper than she already was. Getting married is a huge deal and something that

I want to last a lifetime with my partner. The last thing I wanted was to divorce her afterward."

"Then why do I get the feeling that you're hurting more than you should about this?" Bob asks perceptively. "If your relationship with Claire was as fake as you say, then you shouldn't look like you've lost everything in one fell swoop."

That's when the first of the tears fall. "Maybe because at some point it stopped being fake for me. Maybe when you said we should get married here, I actually contemplated it for the briefest moment."

"Dina." He lets out a huge breath. "Do you know how many times Parker and I have renewed our vows?"

My brows furrow. "I don't understand."

He rolls his eyes and chuckles. "Sometimes, as part of these trips, there's a wedding at the end. It's a way for new resorts or destinations to pivot into a different revenue stream. That's why when you said you had a fiancée...."

"You invited me along."

"Exactly. It saves us another vow renewal. We figured since you two are already engaged, then you can have the wedding."

"But we're not really engaged."

"I don't see what's wrong here. The wedding isn't real either. It wouldn't be legal anyway."

"What?"

"A fake wedding for a fake engagement." He rubs his chin. "There's some humor to it, actually. Parker would be tickled."

"That doesn't matter now."

"And why not?"

I swipe at the pesky tears. "Fake wedding or not, I don't know if Claire feels the same way."

"What makes you say that?"

"She went to Edinburgh without a single look back. If that isn't confirmation that she doesn't feel the same way, then I don't know what is."

Bob shakes his head. "Did you confirm this in any way? Did you ask her how she actually feels?"

"No," I say, defeated.

"Did you tell her how you feel?"

"No."

"Then you can't really be sure, now, can you?" Bob smiles.

A kernel of hope springs inside my chest. "But after the argument we had yesterday? She must hate me."

"Dina, you're a grown woman who knows what she wants. Why should you deprive yourself of loving someone if there's a chance that she loves you back?"

"Then what do I do?"

"Easy. You fly to Edinburgh." Bob picks up the phone. "Good thing we're travel agents, because getting you on a flight is what we do."

I cover my mouth with both hands as I cry in earnest. "Oh, Bob. You're not going to fire me?"

"I don't see why I should," he says while dialing. "Go and bring back Claire. And if she refuses and breaks your heart, know that you still have a job waiting for you. The partnership is still yours."

"Really?" I honestly can't believe what's happening right now.

"Now, will you sign that damn contract and ask the front desk for a car? You have a plane to catch."

When I stand on shaking legs, Bob is already on the phone with the airport, arranging my flight details.

I don't wait another second. I make my way to the front desk.

I have a couple of hours to figure out exactly what I'm going to say to Claire to get her to fall in love with me.

CHAPTER THIRTY

Claire

WHEN DINA said she would get me a slot at the comedy festival, I thought I would perform at one of the smaller venues. I mean, that was really my goal from the beginning. Just to get into one of the smaller venues.

Little did I know that I would be performing on the big stage. The stage where rock stars play when they're in town. I couldn't believe it until I arrived for sound check and the producer ushered me to the center of the stage.

The sweat that comes out of me in that moment is enough to drench my shirt. Good thing for my jacket. The jacket Dina gave me.

Five minutes before I'm about to perform, I take a moment to hyperventilate in the bathroom. Once I catch my breath, I face the mirror and say, "You've been working all these years for this moment, Claire. Now go and murder out there."

Dwight gives my shoulder a smack right as the host calls my name and I step out to the roaring crowd. Many comedians have already come before me, so they are primed. The key is to get them to stay interested.

When I'm in the zone, I begin to pace the stage. Most comics do this because they want to engage with as much of the audience as possible. You want the right side of the room just as attentive as the left.

So you pace like a caged panther. Now, there's a technique to this. You don't want to go too fast, because you will end up making the audience dizzy. Remember, this is a comedy show, not a tennis match.

You don't want to go too slow either. Can you just imagine walking as if you're in slow motion without actually being in slow motion? You're a comedian, not a mime.

Get into a natural rhythm. It's like dancing. You want to follow the steps yet still make your movements your own.

Well, that's what I'm doing right now. I move from right to left on the stage. My muscles are relaxed. My limbs are loose. It's been a while since I've felt this good on stage.

"Do you know what the problem is with being in a relationship?" I say with a harder edge than usual. "It's that you don't know what's going to happen next. See, not that I'm saying I'm in a relationship, because what do I know about those?"

That gets me the starter laughter. The laughter that's willing to go with me on this journey. Not bad. It's new material. I still need to work out the kinks.

"I don't understand why women have a fascination with shopping," I say as I move on to my next joke. "I buy everything from thrift stores, as you can see...." I gesture toward myself, then I realize I'm wearing the jacket Dina bought for me. "Well, not this. This was given to me."

The moment Dina comes to mind, I say, "Actually, the one who gave me this might just have been the best woman to come into my life."

Instead of laughs, I get sighs. Okay, not my best. It falls flat. But I'm not about to give up.

"She actually did this thing that she thought I didn't notice." I pause, making sure everyone is on me. Then I say, "She'd come to bed with makeup on."

That gets me chuckles.

"Oh, she'd pretend she wasn't wearing any, but that only works on guys. Sorry, fellas."

The women laugh as the men grumble.

"I know what mascara looks like, and lips don't shine without a little help from some gloss. Well, I thought to myself, that's fine, she wants to look good while sleeping. Maybe she had a hot date in her dreams."

The roar of laughter I've been waiting for finally comes.

"I wouldn't have thought twice about it until I felt her wake up super early. She didn't think I noticed. I thought she was just going to the bathroom. When she came back, not only had she put on more makeup, she had brushed her teeth too. Boy, did I feel special with my drool on my pillow and my hair sticking out in ways that defy gravity. If she didn't fart in bed, I would have absolutely felt bad for myself."

This time, the men are hooting and hollering.

But I bring it back to earth by saying, "Despite all that, I can't say I don't love her. She's beautiful on the inside and out. And she makes me feel special. Like she really sees me."

"Then why don't you marry her?" someone shouts from the crowd.

I sigh. "Because I'm a total coward. That's why."

Seeing as I'm losing the crowd, and not wanting to fall into a puddle of my own tears, I bring everything back around with another joke.

"Anyway, I dated this girl once who loved to shop. She was so addicted that we'd get packages randomly sent to us. To the point where she didn't even remember having bought the items in the first place."

I get hisses of concern from the audience. Okay, good. I've got their attention again.

"When I asked her about her shopping habit, she had the gall to be angry with me. 'I don't shop that much,' she said, snapping at me. One night, I woke up to find her in the living room with the laptop on. When I asked her what she was doing, she didn't respond. I soon find out that her shopping problem was so bad, she was doing it in her sleep."

I mime clicking on a mouse. "Add to cart. Add to cart. Check out."

That gets me the laugh I'm looking for.

"We broke up soon after that." I pause. "But once in a while, I'll still get a random package in the mail with weird shit inside. I guess she hasn't changed the address on her account yet." Carefully calculated pause. "I always did like her taste in vibrators."

The laughter is like a bomb going off. A shock wave goes through the audience. The energy returns to me, and I absorb it wholeheartedly.

Grinning from ear to ear, I say, "That's it for me tonight. My name's Claire Rox. Thank you, Edinburgh!"

I get off the stage to a standing ovation. I take it all in. This is easily the best night of my life. Probably one of the performances of my life.

I feel so good, I almost want to celebrate, but in the back of my mind, there's only one person I really want to celebrate with.

Dwight comes up to me with a huge scowl on his face. "What was that all about?"

I frown and hike my thumb at the still cheering crowd. "Didn't you just see me kill back there?"

"I saw you messing up. What was that about being in love with someone?"

My defenses go up. "What's it to you?"

"Maybe you're forgetting what your act is all about."

"Dwight, you can go shove my act into your ass," I say, surprising the both of us. "I'm allowed not to be single."

Before Dwight can argue, he's nudged aside as a man comes up to me.

"Claire Rox," he says, reaching out his hand, "my name's Brandon Miller."

"It's nice to meet you," I say, taking his hand. "I don't know if we actually have meet-and-greets for this thing."

"I'm actually a producer over at the Peacock Network," he says. "And I wanted to talk to you about something."

"The Peacock Network. Impressive. I watch a lot of shows from there."

"Thank you for your support." He flashes a wide grin. "Speaking of shows, I actually wanted to talk to you about yours."

I suck in a breath. "What about it?"

"I was watching you tonight and think you're absolutely brilliant."

I feel my cheeks tingle. "Thank you."

"Actually, I was wondering if you would be open to the idea of putting a new spin to your current material."

"What do you mean?"

"Instead of calling it Fun, Fat, and Single, how about Fun, Fabulous, and Married?" Brandon traces an arch in front of me with his hand as if he can see the title on a marquee somewhere.

I'm so taken aback by his suggestion that it takes me a moment to process what he just said. I blink several times. It does have a nice ring to it.

"I can already see this as a show and not just a comedy act on stage," he says, talking rapidly. "My network's been trying to find the right kind of material, and I believe your quirky style is the right one for us."

Again, he leaves me speechless. It takes all of my power not to let my jaw drop and look like a fool in front of him.

"If you'll work with me, I've got so many ideas that I think will fit your style. We can definitely make this into an instant hit. America's been salivating for this kind of content for years with little results. I want to be the first to actually make something that will be successful."

"Wow! I honestly don't know what to say." And it's true.

"You don't have to really say anything. Just listen." He pauses, then says, "I'd like to start putting this project into production. What about this woman you talked about earlier? The one you said you loved?"

I'm taken aback. "About that—"

"Actually, the two of you getting together can be used in the show," he interrupts. "It will be amazing—trust me on this."

I don't know what magic Brandon has, but he has the ability to make you want something you never thought about or never thought you actually wanted. As he speaks, I'm already getting new ideas for material. This kind of excitement hasn't happened to me in a while. I relish the creative jolt it gives me.

"Now it's time for you to say something," he says. I think his speech is done.

"I feel like I just got sold a car" are the first words out of my mouth.

Brandon laughs and wags a finger at me. "That's the kind of comedy gold I'm looking for. We're going to make this happen, Claire. I'm going to make you a star."

"More than I already am?"

"Even more so. All of America will know your name before I'm done with you."

"It's sounds like you're giving me the golden parachute I've been looking for."

"So? What do you think?"

"When you put things that way, I really want to do it." Before he can speak again, I raise a hand to stop him. "But give me time to think about it. I hope you understand that it will be a big leap for me."

"Take all the time you need," he says, when in reality, I know this offer has a time limit. He takes my hand again. "It's such a pleasure meeting you, Claire. I really hope that we can work together. I can see great things happening between us."

"It's nice meeting you too."

"Make sure to send me your agent's information after you've made your decision so that I can give him a call and finalize things."

"I'll do that."

As he walks away, I'm left feeling like a tornado just rushed past me. My mind is spinning with the possibilities. Despite getting my creative juices flowing, Brandon doesn't know that Dina and I might never get back together. Hence there will be no show.

"What did he want?" Dwight asks when he returns to my side.

"Just wanted to say how much he liked my act," I say, the white lie slipping out. Better that way since I don't have the energy to explain anything to Dwight.

"Look, I'm sorry about earlier," he says. "You absolutely have the right to be in a relationship if you want to be. We can make this work. What do you say we celebrate your success tonight?"

"Can we do the celebrating tomorrow?" I ask, happy we can see eye to eye again. "I'm really tired. I didn't get any sleep on the way over here."

"Oh right," Dwight says, full of understanding. "Go back to your hotel and get some rest."

"Thank you."

I watch him walk away. At the moment, I'm stuck like my feet are in fast-drying cement. An opportunity of a lifetime just passed me by, and I was powerless to do anything about it. Just thinking about it makes my stomach tie in knots. I feel a chill run down my spine. It's like I'm coming down with something.

I leave the backstage area and pick up my bag from the greenroom. The adrenaline from the performance high starts to wear off. I walk among the crowd, not really seeing where I'm going.

Chapter Thirty-One

Dina

I WALK and I walk. First I wander around the hotel lobby, waiting for Claire to show up. There are some shops off to the side, so I glance into those, unable to help myself.

Never buy anything at a hotel. It's definitely overpriced. There will always be a similar item in the city you're staying at for much cheaper.

Since window-shopping isn't really my thing and I didn't bring much money anyway, I move away from the stores. I wander into the chocolatier shop and marvel at the different chocolates and macarons they have on offer. The lady at the counter is so nice. She gives me samples to taste.

Each and every piece that I put into my mouth is even better than the last. My eyes pretty much roll into the back of my head when I bite into one that has cherry liqueur inside. I promise her I will come back and buy a box as soon as I withdraw some cash at the closest ATM.

No longer interested in being inside, I find myself heading toward the back garden of the hotel. It's where the fountain is located. It's the view of the restaurant off to the side. The marble is actually quite lovely, depicting women of different sizes all holding jars the water spouts from. Coins litter the fountain floor.

I take a coin out of my purse, make a wish, and toss it in. Now, I know this isn't the Trevi Fountain in Rome, but maybe it has a similar power to grant wishes. There's only one thing I really want in this moment.

I make my way deeper into the garden. I find a stone bench between two lush topiaries in the shape of swans. I sit and lean back against my hands, watching the night sky.

I debated going to the comedy festival when my plane landed, but being there among the chaos didn't seem like the right venue for what I wanted to happen. So instead, I decided to wait for Claire. She's bound to return to the hotel eventually.

The city lights drown out the stars. A pity, since it would have been nice to watch them twinkle. Without my bidding, tears begin to roll down my temples.

I promised myself that I wouldn't cry about this anymore, but seeing Claire in my mind's eye keeps reminding me of what I want. My feelings for her can't just be ignored. No matter how tall the wall I build, those feelings persist.

All it takes is for her to smile at me and I fall in love with her all over again. It's like the legend of Sisyphus. Like the man who is forced to roll a boulder up a hill over and over again, I am condemned to fall in love with Claire each time I see her.

"Dina?" Claire says as if I conjured her out of thin air. "What are you doing here?"

I sit forward and quickly wipe away my tears, but it's too late. She already saw that I was in the middle of crying. The worried look on her face tells me so.

"Wow, that fountain really works," I say under my breath.

"Are you okay?" she asks as she takes a seat beside me.

I move away a little bit, but there's barely any room for me to sit without falling off the bench. I sniff and try not to dry my damn fingers against my dress.

"You're finally here," I say in a clipped tone. "How did you find me?"

"I didn't want to go back to my room right away, so I thought I'd take a walk. At first I didn't think it was you sitting there."

Her tone is so doubtful that I actually laugh. It's a sad sound. It breaks my heart. "Can't a person cry in peace?" I ask, but not of her. Actually, I'm asking no one in particular.

"What happened? Why are you here?"

"Can you just give me a second?" Another wave of these stubborn tears threatens to flow out of my eyes. I look up at the sky again in an attempt to blink them away.

"I'm not leaving until you tell me what's wrong," she says, sounding more determined than I would have liked. There's no way I'm getting rid of her now.

My heart aches as my face crumples. I sniff again. Then I take a deep breath, but that doesn't help in keeping the tears inside. One manages to escape.

"Here," Claire says, handing me something.

I look down to see the white handkerchief with the embroidered daisy that I used to wipe Claire's mouth after she won the pie-eating contest. I take it from her as more tears fall.

"Why do you have this?" I ask, feeling all my walls crumble to dust.

"When the hotel returned it after having it washed, I kept it," she explains. "You never know when you'll need to dry something."

Why is it she never fails to make me laugh?

"You know what?" I begin drying my tears. "I'm sick and tired of this dance."

"I don't understand."

"Fuck it, I don't care what you think." I twist around and face her. "I want you, Claire."

"What?" Her eyes widen as my words sink in.

"For real. No bullshit. I want you."

"Dina...."

I barrel forward because I don't want to chicken out. "There's no point in traveling the world and being happy when I don't have you by my side."

The longest pause in my life happens. I can actually hear crickets chirping in the distance. Then Claire takes my hands and places a kiss on each palm.

"I'm so happy," she says. "You've made me so happy."

This time it's my turn to say, "What?"

She brings my hands to her chest and smiles. "Dina, I feel the same way. I just didn't know how I was going to tell you."

"But what about your show?" I ask, because it's a question that needs clarifying between us for this to work.

"That's what I've been agonizing about." She shakes her head. "Until I realized that it's ridiculous to go on with a show pretending I'm single when I have feelings for you."

"You can't sacrifice your career for me."

"Who says anything about sacrificing my career? In fact, I actually just got an offer to do a show that focuses on me being fun, fabulous, and married."

"Oh my goodness, that's absolutely amazing!" I let go of Claire's hands so I can give her a hug.

"Why did it take so long for us to get to this point?" she asks against my neck.

Lovely shivers run down my spine. "I think this situation is absolutely ridiculous. We should have been honest from the very beginning."

We laugh.

When we regain our composure, Claire stands and reaches out for me. I take her hand and stand as well. We share a smile.

"I'm starving," she says. "Will you have dinner with me?"

"Yes." I nod. "Crying makes me hungry."

We laugh again.

All night long, we enjoy our first official date together. No faking this time. We eat our fill of creamy chicken, the best beef, and the most luscious pork medallions. I think I've gained so much weight on this trip, but I don't care.

Right as we finish eating, Claire says, "Care to join me in my hotel room?"

I lean in, squeeze her thigh suggestively, and whisper into her ear, "I'd join you anywhere you want."

"I'll hold you to that promise," she says just as suggestively.

We're so close I can feel her breath against my lips. All I really want in that moment is to kiss her. To show her what exactly she does to my body by being so close.

"But first," she says as a song starts to play from the house band of the hotel restaurant, "we're going to dance."

She stands and pulls me up with her. With her hand in mine, she leads the way to the dance floor. She's already swaying with each bounce of her step.

Soon we are not the only ones on the dance floor. More couples join us. With each new song that the band plays, we dance, and we laugh the night away.

CHAPTER THIRTY-TWO

Claire

DINA AND I leave the restaurant feeling all warm and fuzzy. The wine we consumed during dinner may have contributed to this feeling We hold hands the entire time we ride the elevator to my floor.

When we get to my room, Dina closes the door firmly behind us, turns the dead bolt, and pulls the chain across. It's dark. Only a touch of light reaches us from a single lamp that I left on in the bedroom down the hall.

I lean back into the wall, looking down at my feet, hands behind me, feeling shyer than I can ever recall being. It seems like an eternity before Dina finally turns to me, slowly, moving into place in front of me. She ducks her head down a little to catch my eye and puts her hand on my chin, tilting my face up toward her.

"Are you sure about this, Claire?"

I can't make my mouth work, so I just nod. Over and over again, like a bobblehead toy on the dash of a car. Finally I whisper, "Yes, I'm sure. For sure."

She smiles a little and looks into my eyes like she's double-checking to be certain. The fact that she's taking her time with me, making sure I'm definite about wanting this, has me twice as aroused as I was before. Her eyes roam over my face, down to my neck, and suddenly I feel so impatient. I want to beg her to do something—anything—to me.

What comes out is a croaky whispered "Please."

She leans in and kisses my forehead. The tip of my nose. Briefest kiss on my lips. One side of my jaw. Near my ear. The side of my neck. I moan and feel my body push into her.

"Please," I manage again.

Her hand comes up slowly, cups one breast through my jacket, the faintest hint of a squeeze, like she's testing the weight and feel of it in her hands. I feel her exhale, hot and damp, against my skin, and it makes me shiver.

"Jesus, Claire, you feel so good," she says. "I want you so badly. I want…. Fuck… I want this to be so good for you."

"It already is," I say and arch my back, pushing my breast deeper into her hand. A small moan escapes my mouth.

That's what snaps Dina's restraint at last. She lifts her mouth to mine and kisses me deep, hard, and her hands come up on either side of my face as her tongue slips into my mouth. I feel new and foolish, like a teenager at my first dance, unsure of what to do. But it only takes a few seconds to catch the rhythm of her kiss, to match her tempo, to surrender my mouth to her tongue's dance. I feel her breathe against my lips, panting now, desperate.

Intuitively, my hips push forward toward her, and wordlessly, without breaking the kiss at all, she pushes her knee forward and up, sliding it between my thighs, pushing up until the top of her knee is against the juncture of my thighs. My body jolts.

"Oh God," I moan out, breaking the kiss.

"Fuck, you're so wet already. I can feel how wet you are through my dress," she replies. She keeps pushing her knee up against me, and I let my weight shift to gain more pressure and traction against her leg.

She slips my jacket off and lets it fall to the floor. She takes the front of my shirt and rips it open, buttons flying everywhere. I unbutton my pants and let them fall to the floor as I kick off my shoes. I stand there in only my underwear as her eyes roam over my body.

"Dina… I need…." I don't know what I need, but I keep saying this, over and over, while rubbing myself against her.

She takes my hand and pulls me behind her down the hall, heading to the bedroom. When we get there, she turns me so I'm backing up against the bed, and I sit down on the edge.

"Dina?" I look up at her, unsure of what to do.

She puts her hands on either side of my face, stroking my hair and cheeks.

"Claire, I've wanted to do this for so long," she says. She leans over, kisses my forehead. "You smell so good. So delicious."

As she's talking, she's pushing me back gently until the challenge of holding myself up hits the tipping point, and I let myself fall backward on the bed. I push back, scooting across the bed to give her room, and she takes the cue, crawling up over me.

She kisses me again, moving from my lips to my neck, to my eyes, and back to my lips over and over. She moves down slightly, her body over mine, and kisses along my shoulders to my chest. She reaches behind me and unsnaps my bra before removing it and throwing it over her shoulder.

She closes her mouth over one nipple and sucks. I almost scream from the feeling of it all. She slowly licks all around my nipple, closing her warm mouth over it again. I moan instantly.

It feels so good, I instinctively squeeze my eyes shut to focus on it. Suddenly her mouth opens wide, sucking in as much of my breast as she can. My hips start to buck, pushing up against her, and she moves her hand down between my legs.

She lifts her head from my breast then, her lips wet and pink, and watches my face as her hand presses between my legs.

"You like it, don't you," she says, her voice deeper, slower.

"Yes," I say, nodding.

I start to close my eyes, but she stops me. "No, keep your eyes open, Claire. I want to watch you."

She moves to my side and kneels on the bed. Her legs are pressed up against me, her eyes pinned on mine, and her hand moving slow and lazy between my legs. I can feel the soft pressure of her fingers moving flat over my panties, and I nudge my hips up into her.

She leans over a little, looking away from my face to gaze down at where she's rubbing me. She lifts her hand off me, takes hold of the edge of my underwear with her fingertips, and moves them to the side.

"Dina," I say, and she looks back to my face. "Please."

She needs no second request. She trails her fingers along my vulva, gently, slowly, slipping between wet lips, opening me. I gasp, and my breathing grows faster, panting.

Her fingers slip deeper, looking for the spot to enter me, and when she finds it, she slips her finger in all the way, easily. The slick, dragging feel is explosively good, and my shoulders lift up off the bed.

She starts a slow rhythm, sliding her finger in and out, and after a moment, she leans over me, her mouth so close I can feel the heat of her breath. She pulls her finger out, and I lift up on my elbows to look at her. She puts her finger in her mouth, tasting me for the first time, and sucks it in and out a few times.

She looks up at me.

"Dina…."

Then she drops her head down onto my pussy, mouth open, tongue flicking, slipping between my lips to find my clitoris. I slide down off my elbows and throw my head back. She licks and sucks, opening her mouth wide over me, playing with me. When she lifts her lips off to take a deeper breath, I instinctively put my hands on her head and lift my hips back up.

"More, Dina…."

She groans, a deep, low growl in her throat. I grip her head tighter, pushing her down. She starts licking me again, furiously now, desperate, fast, needing, and I feel two fingers at my edge again. She pushes them hard into me until she's as deep as she can go, her knuckles up against my lips. She keeps thrusting, the wet sound of her fingers fucking into me a rhythm that she matches with her tongue on my clit.

"I'm going to cum, I'm going to—" and just like that, I cum hard. My thighs close around her head, and my hips buck up against her face again and again.

After what seems like minutes, I finally lay back, my legs open, my breath hitching. She moves up alongside me and kisses me gently. She lays back down next to me, still fully clothed.

I move one of my hands over to her body, slip it between her legs, and touch gently. Her eyebrows pop up and she looks over at me.

"Is it okay if I…."

I let the question trail off, nervous and uncertain again.

"Claire, anything you want to do is so fucking okay it's not even funny."

CHAPTER THIRTY-THREE

Dina

FEELING IT'S unfair that I'm the only one still dressed, I climb off the bed and push the straps of my dress over my shoulders. With nothing left holding the fabric up, it falls to the floor to pool at my feet. I step out of it and kick it aside.

Claire gets on her knees and puts a hand behind my knee. She guides my leg up so my strappy sandal is on the mattress. She reaches behind me, unclasps my shoe, and removes it. She does the same for my other foot.

My cheeks tingle hot when she brings her hand to my face and strokes the corner of my jaw with her impossibly soft thumb. I place my hand over hers, almost instinctively. Our fingers interlock and our lips draw close like magnets dragging us together.

I lose myself in the swirl of the strange, new, familiar softness of her. She smells like a sweet memory. She hooks her fingers over the sides of my panties and pulls them down. I kick those away too.

Once I'm naked and Claire has discarded her underwear, her fingers unravel my nerves as they trail down my back, releasing the frenzied butterflies from the hidden cage door I didn't know existed. I run my fingers up into the thick strands of her hair and pull her gently by the base of her skull further into my kiss. In return, she clutches at my hips to weave me deeper into her world.

Her hand skirts the bare skin of my thigh. The aftershock of my shiver spills out from my tongue into her mouth. She drinks it in like nothing else can ever quench her thirst.

It certainly whets my appetite for more.

Her nimble fingers tease between my legs as I did to her earlier. I pour my gasp down her neck as she traces the line of my slit with torturous care and kisses down the valley between my breasts. When she dips her middle finger between my folds, she's met with a gush of approval.

She slides my slick up to my throbbing clit and traces mindful little circles around and around. The build is blinding as she gradually adds more pressure to her stroke, gauging the intensity of the shocks flitting down my spine, behind my knees, back into her fingers. I bury my face in her shoulder and heave every ounce of air from my lungs to stifle a desperate moan.

As she feels me harden and open into her, she increases the quivering speed of her touch. My mouth leans on the ledge of her collarbone. Then I whip my head back. The cords of my neck strain.

One of my hands grips her hair while the other grasps futilely at the bed. My clit thumps back into her while my hips try to buck her right off. As gradually as she built the pressure, she slows her swirling roll, guiding me back down to her from my pinnacle of bliss.

She pulls back to admire me in my euphoria, but it's as if she's tripped a wire. I lunge at her, taking her down to the bed. Hands first, then lips—expressing my hungry gratitude to her. She bites down on my bottom lip. She then rolls us over, moves to the edge of the bed, and squats down in front of me, looking up at me with her cum-drunk eyes.

I shake my head in an attempt to give a compliment, but I will never find the right words even if I could speak. I run my hand through her hair, down her face. She catches my thumb in her mouth and sucks it in deep, running her tongue along the knuckle. I feel the flick at the base of my spine where it connects with the cool silk of the sheets beneath me.

She pries my knees apart, exposing my pussy to her. My breath is heavy and short all at once in anticipation of her tongue on more of me. Her breath is hot and teasing as she kisses up the length of my inner thigh, ever closer to my aching core.

She flicks me once, twice, between every fold. Sucking in the bud of my clit, she holds it in the warmth of her mouth. My pulse tries to hit the roof of her mouth, but instead I feel it in mine.

The subtle shock urges my eyes open. I admire her tongue as it moves in and out of my field of vision, and notice that though one hand is squeezing my thigh, the other has made its way between her legs. I bite my lip to stifle a groan.

She doesn't skip a beat. She leans to the side and rummages blindly in the bag by the bedside table. When she finds what she's looking for, her lips abandon me. I look at what she's got in her hand and smile.

"Is that…," I whisper. "From the welcome basket?"

A droning buzz fills the room as she turns on the tiny pink vibrator. She brings the rounded edge of the squished egg-like device to where her tongue had just been. She bites my earlobe approvingly at my moan and kisses me again, tongue darting in and out, as she teases at my entrance with one, then two fingers. The tips of her fingers massage my opening while her other hand pushes my clit to the brink. My hips rise in anticipation.

She slides deeper and deeper until she is as far as she can reach with every thrust, curling her fingers up to my belly button every time she slides out. She nibbles at my neck as she drags the orgasm right out of me.

Fingers clutching at the sheets, eyes scrunching, jaw clenching, I tap my head against the mattress beneath me, a little harder each time. My leg starts to twitch violently as my hips fall down following the harsh yet extremely welcome release. Claire presses her lips to mine to distract me from the loss of her fingers, breathing life back into me.

She removes the vibrator from my clit, pressing the little thing silent.

"What other toys do you have in there?" I ask.

Claire leans toward the open bag and removes a couple more vibrators. How many did the chateau staff put in that welcome basket? These are bigger, more phallic, meant to give a wider stretch. My inner walls clench in anticipation.

"Do you want to be on top or the bottom?" she asks.

I take one of the vibrators from her and turn it on. "I like this view better."

"Bottom it is." She turns on her own vibrator.

At first I expect her to put it inside her. Instead, she turns around so her pussy is right above my face. She nudges my legs farther apart and brings the tip to my clit.

I understand what she wants and bring the tip of the vibrator I'm holding to her clit. She draws a circle and I mirror her movements. I show her that she's in charge of this.

She moves the vibrator from my clit to my entrance, but doesn't enter me. What she does is move the toy up and down my pussy lips, coating it with my juices. I do the same. She bucks her hips as I do mine.

Once she feels that I'm ready for her, she inserts the vibrator into me in one slow stroke. I follow suit, inserting the one I'm holding into her at the same snail's pace. Our moans echo each other.

When she pulls out, I pull out. When she thrusts back in, I do the same. It's easy to follow the rhythm she sets for us.

Pretty soon, both our hips are bucking against the thrusts of the vibrators we pull and push in and out of us. As she moves, her nipples rub against my stomach. It adds a layer of sensation that I didn't expect.

I begin to grind into her thrusts as she does with mine. She increases the power of the vibrator, which practically lifts my entire body off the bed in surprise. It takes me a second to do the same for her. She cries out when I finally do.

"I'm close," I say through gritted teeth.

"Me too," she replies. Her lovely juices drip down on me.

We cum within seconds of each other. She's shaking so badly that for a moment I'm scared she will fall over, but she manages to stay where she is. I'm quivering with her, panting hard.

We pull out the vibrators at the same time. Claire uses the last of her strength to turn them both off and set them aside. Then she snuggles up onto my side.

I wrap my arm around her and kiss the top of her head. Her breathing calms, as does mine. I don't even remember the last time I've cum this hard nor felt this good afterward.

CHAPTER THIRTY-FOUR

Claire

DINA AND I sit at the back of an SUV that Bob is driving. Parker sits in the passenger seat. They volunteered to pick us up from the airport when we arrived back in Paris. A part of me misses the Bentley, but hey, what can I say?

I honestly think in the back of Bob's mind, he wants to make sure we actually go through with this wedding. Of course, that's the paranoid side of me. Between packing stints, Dina and I haven't stopped having sex, so it's safe to say we're not going anywhere without each other any time soon.

I'm looking out the window. Dina slips her hand into mine and interlocks our fingers. I look toward her and she gives me a kiss on the cheek. She's such an affectionate person. I just love soaking in what she's willing to give me.

"You two are so lovey-dovey," Parker gushes. "I never once believed you were faking. It looks so natural for you two to be together."

We both blush and look out our separate windows, but our hands remain intertwined. I can't wait to get this honeymoon started.

Dina, as I expected, became a total packing dictator. In the end, I gave her free rein of my suitcase just to save us the aggravation of bickering.

It doesn't matter that I've been on more planes than her. She's the expert in packing. Sure. Some battles you just need to concede to make a relationship work. It will make a good joke, though.

"You two excited?" Bob asks as we pull up to the driveway of the chateau.

"Been excited since you offered me this opportunity," Dina says.

I give her hand a reassuring squeeze. There's no stopping us now. She's getting this promotion and I'm taking that show deal. Everything is on the up-and-up for us.

When we reach the entryway, we all get out of the SUV. The line of staff once again moves into action, grabbing our luggage. Parker runs off to make what I assume are final preparations for the wedding that's about to happen. Dina and I just stand there, calm among the organized chaos. Bob leaves the keys with the valet, then saunters off into the chateau.

"We have everything ready for you," Pullen says when she reaches us.

"Isn't the wedding already ready?" I ask, totally naïve. I just want to get this over with already.

She lets out a soft laugh. "What I mean is, there is a dress waiting for you," she says to Dina. "And there's a suit waiting for you," she says to me.

"A dress?" Dina asks.

"Everything has been taken care off," Pullen adds. "We even have a makeup team for the both of you."

"Got to look good for those pictures," I say, knowing the show might want to buy the rights from the chateau. Just thinking of it makes me giddy. Dwight was beside himself when I told him everything.

Another two staff members approach us.

"They will take you to your rooms to get ready." Pullen gestures toward her colleagues.

"Can't we get ready together?" Dina looks to me.

"Right," I say, taking her hand. "We're not ready just yet to be separated, you see."

"That is highly unusual." Pullen purses her lips for a moment. Then she smiles. "But I believe that we can accommodate you."

"Thank you." I smile at her before placing a kiss on the top of Dina's hand.

We follow the trio into the chateau. At first I think we're heading upstairs. Instead, they lead us into a sitting room that's been converted into a salon. Dina is ushered into one chair, and I'm pointed to the one beside her.

The amazing thing is, no matter how many hands run over us to get us ready, Dina and I sit calmly through it all. I get the girl. I get another vacation. And I get the career to boot? It's almost too overwhelming to think about.

Hair takes an hour. Makeup takes even more. Thank goodness for the patience of my makeup artist, because I can't keep my eyes open long enough for her to apply a proper coat of mascara.

Pullen saunters back into the room with a couple of dress bags in her hands.

"Is that my dress?" Dina asks, excitement in her eyes.

She nods. "Yes. Brought here from an atelier in Paris."

"Oh! I think I'm going to cry," she says, fanning her face.

"Don't you dare," Pullen warns. "We do not have time to reapply your makeup."

Apparently Pullen can be quite the taskmaster. She keeps everyone on our toes. When she commands, the staff jumps to do her bidding. I'm totally impressed.

"So, we're getting married," I say as I take a careful sip from the straw of the ginger ale I asked for from the bar. "It's totally surreal."

"Well, believe it, because it's happening." Dina smiles at me. "I'm not letting you go."

I believe her. "Ditto. Tell me about this honeymoon we're going on after this."

"Well, it's a twenty-two-hour flight to Sydney," she begins. "Then we switch to a smaller plane that will take us to Vanuatu."

"I've never heard of it," I say. "It must be amazing if Bob picked it for us."

She blushes, then nods. "It's actually going to be my first assignment as well. It's all already arranged."

"How are you liking being a full-fledged partner now?" I ask, genuinely excited about this next phase in our lives.

"Sometimes I have to pinch myself to actually make sure I'm not dreaming." She sighs. "We're going to have to get a bigger place in New York."

"Let's talk about that when we actually get back," I say, leaning against my seat and letting the makeup artist continue to do her thing.

"But you know how I like to prepare."

"I do, my love, but let's not spoil the vacation with thoughts of moving in together." When she pouts, I correct myself. "Do you honestly want to spend our entire honeymoon thinking about apartment shopping?"

She looks sheepish when she says, "It's a long flight with free Wi-Fi."

"Are you saying you want to look at apartments while we're thirty thousand feet off the ground?"

"Yes?"

We look at each other and laugh, but I know Dina is serious. If I don't look at apartments with her during our flight and have a list of listings to look at by the time we get back, she'll sulk the entire time.

"As long as I'm allowed to make this into a joke in the future, then I'll look at apartment listings with you," I tease, but she knows I'm serious.

Everything is fair game when you're about to marry a comedian. Dina doesn't mind. We know how to laugh at ourselves. In fact, we constantly laugh at how we got into this situation.

"One day this will make a great story to tell our kids," she says.

"As long as you carry them, then I don't have a problem with that."

"How about you carry one and I carry one?"

"How about we get a surrogate instead?"

"I get it—it's a bigger discussion for another time."

We look at each other for the longest time before we laugh again. There are so many decisions to make in blending our lives together. Thank God we have our entire lives to make them.

"As long as we talk things through, no matter the argument we have, we'll be okay," she says.

"We'll definitely be okay." I take her hand and kiss the top of it again. It's become my favorite thing to do.

Pullen announces that we're ready to start getting dressed. My heart jumps to my throat. This is it. This is the beginning of our forever together.

"Oh!" I say, startling Dina and everyone else in the room.

"What?"

"I almost forgot." I pull out a small box from my pocket and hand it to her.

"What's this?" She looks at it.

"Just some jewelry to seal the deal," I say.

She opens the box and sees the two-karat diamond ring inside.

"Claire!" She says my name as a gasp. "Where did you get that?"

"Pawn shop." She smiles indulgently. "It's vintage."

"That time you said you were going to get breakfast?" I smile back. "We really need to train you out of this buying secondhand thing."

"Admit it, you love that about me."

Dina rolls her eyes. I'm so right, but apparently she will not be an enabler by agreeing with me.

"Dina Oliver, will you marry me, officially?" I ask her.

"Yes!" she says a little too loudly.

We kiss to the applause of the entire chateau staff in the sitting room.

CHAPTER THIRTY-FIVE

Dina

AFTER SPENDING two hours on a plane, even if it's first class, and two hours in the car getting to the chateau, the last thing I expected was for Claire and I to get whisked away. The wedding is actually happening. Parker and Bob are making double sure of it.

To say I'm excited to be spending the rest of my life with Claire is a total understatement. I finally found the one for me. The one person who makes me laugh and who makes me want to be a better person. I think that's the most important thing.

Claire got dressed before I did and has already gone down to the garden to see if everything's set up. She said I should take my time getting ready and that she wanted to see me when I was already in my dress. That gave me all the warm and fuzzies.

With the help of Pullen, I shimmy into my dress. She zips it up without any trouble. I look at myself in the mirror and try not to tear up again.

The dress has a vintage feel to it, which is all the rage on the runways right now. It's made of the softest lace and flows when I move. The sleeves billow out and tie at the wrist.

The hairdresser places some finishing touches on my hair, which is up in an intricate bun at the back of my head. A net of pearls secures every strand there. I feel like a princess.

I'm wearing wedges because I'll be walking on grass. I thank Pullen for thinking ahead and not putting me in stilettos that will surely skewer into the lawn. But even if she did put me in stilettos, all I care about is getting married to Claire. I pick up my bouquet of orchids. It goes well with all the white I'm wearing.

I leave the sitting room we used to get ready and make my way down to the garden. Pullen trails after me, holding my train so that it doesn't drag on the ground. We opted for no veil because I want an unobstructed view when I walk down the aisle.

I can see the pristine water of the lake from where I stand, and I smile. Memories of our first kiss at the shore of that lake come back to me. There are so many beautiful places in this world, and I'm glad to be in one of them. It fills my heart with so much love to be getting married here.

"Are you ready?" Pullen asks, teary-eyed.

"Thank you, Pullen, for all your help," I say.

"A wedding is a beautiful thing." She takes my hand. "It brings together two souls and makes them one. It is said that when two people marry, two stars in the sky come together and shine as one."

"That's so beautiful, Pullen. Thank you for sharing it with me."

"Everything is ready. I shall take you there."

She takes my hand and leads me toward a path lined with flowers on each side. There are torches too, but I believe they will be lit later, after the sun sets. Right now, the sun is low in the sky, painting everything a golden orange hue.

The band is playing "Can't Help Falling in Love" as a local woman sings the song, but in French, which gives it a lyrical, magical quality. Ahead of me stands a local pastor Bob hired to officiate. By now Claire has told him that we will be exchanging our vows.

And Claire. She stands to the right of the pastor in a cream-colored linen suit, a necklace of orchids around her neck.

The moment she sees me, she gasps in surprise. I lock gazes with her the entire time I walk down the grassy path lined with flower petals. I can feel myself tearing up, but I do my best to hold my emotions in.

When I reach Claire, Pullen takes the bouquet from me and stands aside. Claire takes both my hands and looks into my eyes. I see unending love on her face.

"You look beautiful," she whispers.

"You look just as beautiful," I say.

"And here I thought I couldn't love you any more than I did a moment ago. Let's get this over with so I can show you my appreciation."

I gasp. "Not in front of the pastor!"

We both look at him in apology, and he merely smiles before he says, "Are you ready?"

We nod.

To those gathered—mostly the chateau staff and all the couples from the different agencies—he says, "Today is a celebration. A celebration of love, of commitment, of friendship, and of two people who are in it for forever. This place represents the endless supply of love that is present, and while at times things may get wild and woolly like crashing waves, your love, like the lake, is always present, and calm will come again."

My heart grows several sizes larger as Claire squeezes my hands. We are doing this. We are actually doing this.

The pastor continues by saying, "You fell in love by chance, but you're here today because you're making a choice. You both are choosing each other. You've chosen to be with someone who enhances you, who makes you think, makes you smile, and makes every day brighter. Claire and Dina, make your promises to one another."

We face each other, and Claire takes a deep breath before she says, "Dina, I love you. Today, I give myself to you in marriage. I promise to encourage and inspire you, to laugh with you, and to comfort you in times of sorrow and struggle. I promise to love you in good times and in bad, when life seems easy and when it seems hard, when our love is simple, and when it is an effort. I promise to cherish you and to always hold you in the highest regard. These things I give to you today, and all the days of our life."

I barely hold back the tears as I say, "Claire, from this day forward, I promise you these things. I will laugh with you in times of joy and comfort you in times of sorrow. I will share in your dreams and support you as you strive to achieve your goals. I will listen to you with compassion and understanding, and speak to you with encouragement. I will remain faithful to our vows for better or for worse, in times of sickness and health. I will love and respect you always."

"You've both chosen to wear rings as a reminder of these promises," the pastor says. "Please exchange rings."

Claire places the gold band around my finger to join the engagement ring she gave me earlier. I place a similar gold band on her finger. Then we both look at the pastor.

"May your marriage bring you all the exquisite excitements a marriage should bring." He smiles. "By the power vested in me by God, I now pronounce you partners in life and love. You may now kiss each other."

As tears fall from our eyes, Claire takes my face in both her hands. She leans closer and I lean forward. We meet in the middle in the sweetest kiss.

Everyone around us cheers and showers us with petals. We break the kiss to laugh. Then Claire takes my hand and we walk back down the aisle.

Our reception is held by the lake. The chateau threw a party in our honor, which, I suspect, Bob and Parker had a hand in too. Claire and I sit at a table of honor.

The guests at the chateau come one by one to us and express their congratulations. They are strangers, but they are happy for us, which makes us all the happier. We eat our fill, then dance for what seems like hours.

Once the moon has risen, Claire and I take a walk along the lakeshore. We're hand in hand. I'm by the water, the waves slashing gently against my bare feet.

"Are you happy?" Claire asks.

"What a strange question," I say. "Of course I'm happy. I'm so happy that I could almost burst with it."

"Good, because I feel the same way." She grins. "I just wanted to make sure."

"When we first met, did you ever think we would get to this place? Actually be married?"

"I fell in love with you the second you gave me that jacket," she says. "I just didn't know it was love then. I just knew I couldn't be without you."

I take those words to heart. I stop walking and wrap my arms around Claire's shoulders. I show her just how much I love her with a kiss that seems to last forever.

Keep reading
for an excerpt from
the F/F paranormal mystery
Dead Woman's Pond
by Elle E. Ire

FEMALE BOWLERS have balls.

I smooth down the peeling sticker on my bag and set the double-sized bowling ball carrier on the floor beside one of the bar's lower tables. I plop myself on the metal chair with the torn vinyl seat and tug off first one mud-encrusted work boot, then the other. The neon signs on the walls flicker through the haze of cigarette smoke, making my eyes water. Spilled beer puddles on the table's surface.

Reaching to the side, I bang the heels of the boots against the inner rim of the garbage can, knocking off the day's dried muck. Could've just used the black-and-gray-checkered linoleum floor, but the waitress and the bartender are friends of mine. No need to make more work for them.

Out of my bag I pull bowling shoes, a used pair bought from this very alley the year they upgraded to new ones. Hey, when you find a set that fits, you hang on to them. They slide onto my feet like my most comfortable bedroom slippers—if I owned bedroom slippers.

"How about a beer, Flynn? We've got a couple of new microbrews on tap."

I glance up from tying the laces, pulling my dirty-blonde ponytail out of my face and throwing it over my shoulder to hang halfway down my back. Allie stands beside the table, order pad in one hand and pen in the other. Not like she needs either one, but she says they're her version of a security blanket. My eyes trail up her long, shapely legs in the way-too-short miniskirt the manager makes her wear. A white button-down blouse hangs open almost to her belly button, where she has the tails tied in a knot.

Strictly look but don't touch. Steve, the bartender, is her boyfriend, and they make a great couple.

"Hey, Allie," I return. She prefers Allison, but everyone calls her Allie because, hey, she works in a bowling alley, and she's certainly never heard that one before. She gave up fighting it long ago. My thoughts shift to the handful of change and a few crumpled singles in my pocket—enough money for the lunch truck at the construction site tomorrow and one game. "Um, gonna have to pass on the beer. I'd love some water, if you don't mind me hogging up a table." I gesture toward the bar's exit opening out to the lanes.

Allie pops her gum. The faint scent of peppermint carries across the space between us. She makes a show of scanning the bar. Two old guys on stools at the counter. Four ladies in matching team shirts around a table on the far side, a half-dozen empty Bud Lites between them. Dave and Charlie, a couple of guys in their forties, guys I've seen before and occasionally bowled against, take up two other seats, doing exactly what I'm doing: putting on shoes, strapping on wrist support bands, wiping their sweaty fingers with rosin bags out of habit rather than current need, or applying New-Skin to old cuts and scrapes.

Lots of empty tables.

I pull out my own New-Skin bottle, almost empty, and open it. The pungent antiseptic odor rocks me back in my seat until a hand wave clears the air. A couple of dabs seal over a cut on my thumb I got when my saw slipped this morning.

"Oh yeah, I'm really swamped," Allie says. "Don't know how I'll manage all the orders." She holds out her empty notepad for me to see, then flips the chair opposite me around and straddles it, her twirly miniskirt draping to either side and barely covering the tops of her thighs. I swallow and focus on tightening my wrist support band. She leans her arms across the seat back. "Tapped out again?"

I work up a lopsided grin for her. "It'll be okay. New job—that apartment complex going up in Festivity. Steady work for over a month now, but I'm still living paycheck to paycheck. We went a long time before the company got this contract, none of the others were hiring temps, and I don't get paid again until day after tomorrow." I glance around at the pitiful prospects Kissimmee Lanes has to offer tonight. "That's why I'm here, actually." When I'd much, much rather be in a hot shower. I worked the site all day in Florida's famous ninety-plus heat and stayed three extra hours off the clock to help my foreman and friend, Tom, with the paperwork. Every muscle in my body aches, and my head hurts from dehydration.

Allie follows my thoughts. "Doesn't look good. Everyone here knows you, even if you've been avoiding us lately."

I pout at her.

She tucks the pen behind her ear and reaches across to pat my shoulder. I suppress a wince. Took a loose board to that shoulder this afternoon, and the bruise will be a beaut. "I know you aren't really hiding from us," she says. "Believe me, I understand 'broke.' Maybe you'll get lucky. We've had some newbies over the past few weeks." Allie pulls the bar rag from her waistband and wipes down the table, then stands. "Hang in there. I'll grab you some water." She flounces off, her skirt flipping up a little when she turns, revealing black boy-shorts underneath.

Oh yeah, I'll look plenty.

In the lanes area, it's all family friendly. If Allie goes out there to take orders, she buttons a few more shirt buttons and is careful not to bend over. In the bar, it's all about the guys and the tips.

"You hoping to pick up a game?"

The shadow that falls across my table is wide, the voice a rich baritone, but the grin on the sunburned, freckled face seems genuine enough. I gesture at the chair Allie abandoned. "Maybe. What's the bet?"

He's a little older, this big hulk of a man who takes a cautious seat as if he's worried it might collapse beneath him. Given the way the metal squeaks in protest, it just might. Late twenties, shaggy brown hair, all muscle, no fat on his body. His biceps strain the fabric of the white cotton T-shirt he wears. He drops a double-ball bag beside him; the equipment rattles inside, and the polyurethane balls clonk against each other with a familiar resonance.

Lots of strength in his arms. Two bowling balls. Personal gear. He takes the game seriously. Invests money in it. Doesn't mean he averages high, but….

My mind screams *bad bet*, but I need the cash. My truck's gas gauge arrow teeters on empty. Can't collect a paycheck if I can't drive to work the next two days. I'm lucky today happens to be Wednesday—the night Kissimmee Lanes hosts unofficial pickup games and bets quietly change hands to the winners.

If my girlfriend, Genesis, were here, she could ask the spirit world about the guy's skills. My lips curl upward. Gen works as a psychic, gets paid well for it, and probably wouldn't appreciate me asking her for something so trivial. She takes her job seriously, even if I don't necessarily believe everything she thinks she does. She believes in it, and I believe in her.

"Lady's choice," the guy says, scanning me as well and bringing my thoughts back to the current decision—the bet and how much. Right. He glosses over my face, eyes lingering on my upper arms and the muscles there. I'm not ripped or anything, not defined like a bodybuilder or weightlifter, but hauling tools, cinder blocks, and bags of cement mix around keeps me in good shape. His once-over ends on my open bag and the solitary blue bowling ball beside the boots I carefully tucked inside it.

That ball cost me a hundred and sixty bucks, custom-drilled to fit my hand and the odd double-jointedness of my right thumb, and worth every penny. I've had her since college. She's gotten some nicks and scratches, had a couple of repairs, but she's served me well.

"Let's say, twenty?" I offer, biting my lower lip. I don't have twenty dollars, not on me and not in the bank. If I lose, I'll have to borrow from Steve and Allie. That will suck, but it won't be the first time, and I always pay them back.

God, once upon a time I made a good annual salary, owned a condo, drove a decent car. Now… I shake off the pity party and focus.

Normally I'd go for fifty, but I don't know this guy. The other scattered players watch our interaction. Charlie grins at me from his table. Dave snickers into his rum and Diet Coke.

I can't tell if they're laughing at me or at my would-be opponent. They certainly won't drop me any hints about his skill level, considering how many times I've kicked their asses over the years.

My companion's eyebrows rise. "Twenty, huh? You sure about that, honey?"

Honey? "On second thought, let's make it thirty."

He holds out his hand, a wide smile spreading across his face. "Thirty it is."

Shit, I just got played. I roll my eyes ceiling-ward and smile back so he knows I'm aware of it. And willing to accept the consequences of my egotistical stupidity.

"I'm Kevin. Kevin Taylor."

Taylor. Taylor. Why do I know that name?

Then it hits me. The trophy case next to the shoe rental desk. First Place Team Captain, 2008. Perfect 300 Game, 2007.

"Flynn Dalton." I accept the handshake. His swallows mine in a firm, self-assured grip.

Oh, I'm so screwed.

EVA MUÑOZ loves dreaming of worlds filled with hot guys falling in love with each other. She believes that love is love is love and everyone has a right to find their person. Her love for writing began in high school. It was because her teacher complimented a story she had written that put her on the path she is on today. She would spin yarns on her father's electric typewriter, bind the pages together, and bring the finished product to school for her classmate to pass around and swoon over. Little did she know at the time that writing would be a career she never knew she wanted.

She may have taken a circuitous path toward her passion for writing, but when she finally made that decision to stick with it after countless rejections, she never looked back. A degree in creative writing helps too. When she's not at her favorite coffee shop thinking up new worlds and characters to explore, you can find Eva in a classroom teaching creative writing of all things. Talk about passion meets day job. Today she is molding impressionable minds the way her teacher once did for her.

For more
great fiction
from

DSP PUBLICATIONS

visit us online.

WWW.DSPPUBLICATIONS.COM

* 9 7 8 1 6 4 1 0 8 3 2 5 6 *